THE WANTED BRIDE

BY SYLVIA MCDANIEL

Books by Sylvia McDaniel

Contemporary Romance

Standalones
The Reluctant Santa
My Sister's Boyfriend
The Wanted Bride
The Relationship Coach
Her Christmas Lie
Secrets, Lies, and Online Dating
Paying for the Past
Cupid's Revenge

Anthologies
Kisses, Laughter & Love
Christmas with you

Collaborative Series

Magic, New Mexico
Touch of Decadence

Western Historicals

Standalones
A Hero's Heart
A Scarlet Bride
Second Chance Cowboy

The Cuvier Women
Wronged
Betrayed
Beguiled

Lipstick and Lead
Desperate
Deadly
Dangerous
Daring
Determined
Deceived

Scandalous Suffragettes
Abigail
Bella
Callie
Faith

The Burnett Brides
The Rancher Takes a Bride
The Outlaw Takes a Bride
The Marshal Takes a Bride
The Christmas Bride

Anthologies
Wild Western Women
Courting the West
Wild Western Women Ride Again

Collaborative Series

The Surprise Brides
Ethan

American Mail Order Brides
Katie

The Wanted Bride
Published by Virtual Bookseller

Cover Design by Kim Killion
http://thekilliongroupinc.com/

Edited by Andrea Dickinson
http://www.qualitybookservices.com/

Formatted by Laurelle Procter
laurelleprocter@gmail.com

Short Description: Valerie Burrows is running from a past life – a past fiancé, to be specific – and Matt Jordan has far too much in common with that man, including the desire to marry her.

ISBN: 978-1-942608-40-0 (paperback)
ISBN: 978-1-942608-41-7 (e-book)

{Contemporary Romance – Fiction}
{Romance – Fiction}

www.SylviaMcDaniel.com

Synopsis

She's a Runaway Bride
Valerie Burrows is running from a wedding, her attorney fiancé, and the law. Pampered Valerie takes a bus to nowheresville, where she learns her cash and credit cards have been stolen. Left with only her designer clothes and luggage she takes on a new identity and must learn to be self-reliant. She swears off men, especially attorneys, only to find the one man who refuses a one night stand and wants a relationship.

He's Looking For A Wife
Matt Jordan, the Colorado Crusher, is the most successful liability lawyer in the state. After the death of his brother-in-law, he realizes he's ready to settle down with a family of his own. His only requirements are intelligent, great-looking, wants more than a hook-up, and doesn't lie. After witnessing the lies his father told his mother, he demands complete honesty. Yet Valerie Brown shows him sometimes in order to find yourself, you must become someone else. Even if that means lying.

Table of Contents

Chapter One

"I need a one-way ticket to anywhere," Valerie Burrows commanded the girl behind the bus counter in downtown Dallas. A charred piece of her wedding veil sagged onto her face. Impatiently, she flipped the singed lace away, her throat closing off the tears that threatened her vision.

On what was supposed to be the happiest day of her life, she reeked of smoke, not flowers, saw red not white, tasted bile not cake.

Glancing up from the counter the clerk's eyes widened, making Valerie acutely aware of her appearance. On what was supposed to be the happiest day of her life, she felt traumatized, not joyous.

"Whe...re do you want to go?" the clerk stammered.

"Anywhere, as long as I leave in the next five minutes," Valerie insisted, wishing people would stop staring. So she looked like a crazy woman. After this morning maybe she was a little loco.

"The bus to Amarillo is loading now," the agent advised, her large brown eyes riveted to Valerie. "I have one seat left. The one-way fare is sixty-five dollars."

Though she preferred to travel by plane, there was no time or way to get to the airport. She could take the bus or stay and face the consequences of her actions.

Valerie dug the cash out of her Bottega Veneta purse and handed the money to the ticket agent. "I'll take it."

Dirty lace from her wedding veil fell onto her face again, so she yanked the offending garment off her head and threw the veil on top of her matching Louis Vuitton luggage.

The beautiful lace of her Vera Wang wedding gown was streaked with gray and black. Burn streaks made a crazy pattern on the silk that didn't accessorize the seed pearls.

The heel of one of her Stuart Weitzman pumps had snapped several blocks ago, and her feet were blistered. And yet her heart beat on in spite of her ruined wedding.

The clerk handed her the ticket, sympathy in her dark eyes. "The bus is ready. You're the last one to board."

Not even time to change. Head held high, spine locked in place, she limped to the white steel carriage, her suitcases trailing behind.

There, she handed her two suitcases to a gawking young man. He opened his mouth to speak, but she held up her hand. "Just load my luggage."

She glanced up to see faces pressed against the glass windows of the bus, gaping at her like she was a freak show.

Hadn't these people ever seen a runaway bride in real life before? Julia Roberts may have made the movie, but she didn't own the copyright to wedding disasters.

With her carry-on bag hanging from her shoulder, Valerie marched up the steps of the waiting bus as if she walked around in a wedding gown every day. The babble of sixty voices ceased as she handed the driver her ticket.

He mumbled, "Lord, I need to retire."

Her silk dress pressed against her legs and swished as she made her way to the only empty seat on her getaway bus. Thank God she'd ditched the petticoats in the Corvette.

A gray-haired woman glanced at her as she put her luggage in the overhead bin.

"Hm hm hm, I can't wait to hear this story," the elderly Hispanic woman said. "Are you all right?"

Valerie plopped in the seat, her ruined silk gown making a mighty swish. She exhaled loudly, her heart aching, her eyes blurring with unshed tears. For the last hour she'd been holding her breath while making her escape.

But now, now all the pain she'd carefully controlled broke free and she chuckled. Hysterical laughter rumbled from deep inside her, echoed through the bus. A single tear rolled down her cheek.

"I am now."

~

In forty-eight hours a girl's life could change completely. Valerie stepped off the bus in the small town of Springtown, Colorado. Population 294. *Salute!*

In Amarillo she'd bought a ticket to Denver and pitched her wedding gown in the trash. After sitting beside a drug dealer all the way to Albuquerque, being proposed to by a parolee on the way to Santa Fe, and awakening to an elderly woman riffling through her Louis Vuitton carry-on, it was time to ditch public transportation. She'd take a taxi to the nearest car rental place and continue her journey in her own set of wheels.

The air brakes hissed as the driver released them, and the bus pulled away from the depot, which consisted of a bench in front of a café. The cold wind whipped right through her thin clothes as she stood alone on the street.

She pushed open the door to the small diner. A "Help Wanted" sign banged against the glass. The greasy spoon was filled to capacity in the late evening, but suddenly her stomach growled, reminding her of the Snickers bar she'd eaten in Albuquerque was not a five-course meal.

The café grew quiet as Valerie pulled her luggage across the wooden floor, the wheels thump, thump, thumping. She sat down, sighing in relief, and the chatter resumed. She desperately needed a latte grande.

A woman with stained white sneakers and a food splattered dress stopped at her booth.

"What can I get you?" she asked.

"I'd like eggs Benedict with a skim, no whip, pumpkin spice latte. Make it a grande."

The waitress glanced at her matching luggage.

"Honey, I think you must have missed your bus stop. This here is Springtown, not Vail. I'm not Martha Stewart, and I don't do lattes."

Valerie frowned and bit back the quick retort that sprang to her lips. Had the woman never heard of Starbucks?

"What do you have?" she asked, wondering if the bus had dropped her off on Mars, or if she was starring in her own personal *Twilight Zone* episode.

"Did you look at the menu?"

"No."

"I'd suggest you start there," the waitress said.

"Give me two eggs over easy, with coffee." Valerie replied. "Do you have any hazelnut cream to go in the coffee?"

"Here in Springtown our cows don't produce flavors." She pushed her pen back behind her ear. "My name is Fran if you need anything else."

The waitress hurried off. Valerie gazed around the café and noticed the sheriff and a guy whose dark looks would normally have taken her breath away occupied a booth across the room. However, in the last forty-eight hours she'd sworn off men. Today her heart pounded a little harder, but only because the sheriff sat across from the tall, dark, handsome man. Surely two states away no one would be searching for her.

Yet.

With the number of criminals loose in this world, why would law enforcement be interested in a good girl with a temporary case of wedding insanity from Dallas? Her crime was minor compared to the act of her two best friends. Or since they'd betrayed her, were they really her friends?

Lonely and weary and sad, Valerie stared at the menu. Her mind reeled, unable to comprehend the idea that her own father had taken Carter's side. She swallowed hard to keep the tears at bay.

A thousand miles away and still her mind staggered from the pain of their betrayal.

The waitress brought her plate of eggs and set them on the table. Her stomach rolled as the smell of fried bacon smacked her in the face.

"Two eggs over easy with a side of bacon."

"No meat!" Valerie grimaced at the greasy bacon, her stomach clenching a warning signal.

The waitress reached down and with her fingers scooped the bacon off the plate.

Valerie gasped. She wasn't in Dallas anymore.

"Two eggs over easy without bacon. Anything else?"

The sooner she got out of this one-horse town, the better. "Yes, where is the nearest car rental office?"

The waitress laughed as fear spiraled along Valerie's spine. Somehow this couldn't be good.

"Honey, who are you visiting in town?"

"No one. Why?"

She gazed at Valerie's luggage.

"You just got off that bus, right?"

"Yes."

"Did you know where you were when you got off?"

"Not really. I couldn't take the people on the bus any longer and decided to rent a car."

The waitress shook her head. "Sugar, the nearest car rental place is in Denver, and you're a good two hours from there. The next bus stops here on Wednesday. Until then, you can cool your heels at the Springtown Inn. It's old, but the rooms are clean."

"There's no car rental place in this town?" she asked in

disbelief, needing to confirm she'd heard correctly.

The waitress chuckled. "No. We barely have a stop light."

Valerie felt like someone had just kicked her in the shin. She had no choice. She refused to call her father and give him the satisfaction of knowing she'd fallen on her face again. Besides, he was furious with her and would tell Carter her whereabouts. By now they'd probably found Carter's beloved car. Or what was left of it. She was stuck in Nowhereville with no cell phone and no one to call for help. Not even her ex-best friend, Blair.

Valerie practiced her yoga breathing to control the panic rising within her. She was an adult. She had a college education. She could take care of herself. She would get through this.

Maybe being in such a small town wasn't a bad thing after all. Who would search for her here?

A couple of days in a hotel room could be time spent deciding what to do with the rest of her life. She could get a massage, maybe a pedicure. She would survive.

Quickly, she finished her eggs and sipped at the rank coffee that didn't even change color after five creamers. She expected fuzz to appear on her chest at any moment.

The waitress laid the check on her table.

"Hey, sheriff, you want any more coffee?" she yelled across the room.

"No thanks, Fran. I need to get on the road."

"You goin' to chase some dangerous criminals?" the waitress teased.

"Nah, Charlie's cows are out again," the man in uniform responded.

"How about you, Matt?" she asked the man sitting across the table, the one who seemed more like a suit and tie kind of guy. His looks were rugged yet refined. "More coffee, or you gotta get back to your lawyering?"

Her last nerve sizzled on high alert.

Another lawyer! Don't give him a second glance, she thought.

"Not tonight," he answered. "I spent the day with McKenzie helping her with the kids."

Was Valerie sick, or did she only appreciate men who were creative with the truth? Was she a lawyer magnet only drawn to cheats and liars? She couldn't seem to clear their magnetic field.

"I'm sure you spoiled those kids good," Fran said.

"Every chance I get," the man replied.

The urge to run all but overwhelmed Valerie. The legal network of lawyers was widespread, and her father well known. He'd find her, and she needed a much deserved break from the drama. She had to leave before she had a panic attack.

She reached into her purse to grab her wallet and pay for her meal.

Her fingers dug to the bottom of her designer purse trying to locate her wallet. Nothing.

She threw back the leather flap, and instead of feeling she started frantically digging, searching for the matching leather wallet that contained her life. The thousand dollars in cash, three credit cards, her driver's license, her very identity.

Instead she found her Ralph Lauren sunglasses, her Lancôme lipstick, her keys, her Monte Blanc pen, and her Estee Lauder perfume.

Everything except her wallet.

Panic squeezed her chest and her breathing became shallow and tight. Oh God, could her life get any worse? The old woman must have done more than rifle through Valerie's luggage. She must have stolen the wallet.

Stolen just like Blair had taken Carter.

She was stuck in Springtown, Colorado, with no money

and no credit cards. She couldn't even pay the five-dollar check, and a lawyer and the town sheriff sat across the way. She gasped for breath, needing more oxygen.

The waitress looked in her direction and gave her a puzzled frown.

How did one sneak out the door without paying while lugging two big suitcases? Valerie tried to stand, but her legs refused to cooperate. Her heart pounded in her chest, and the edges of her vision darkened like the closing credits of a show. With sickening certainty she knew she was going to faint.

Dear God, she was going to faint right in front of the two people she didn't want to notice her! With that she crumpled to the floor around her Louis Vuitton luggage.

~

Something was terribly wrong. Excited voices seeped into her mind, and the stringent smell of Pine-Sol stole her breath, leaving her coughing and sputtering.

"Stand back and give her some air," a vaguely familiar voice said.

"Does she need CPR? I've been trained in CPR," a man said from a distance.

Oh God, it hadn't been a nightmare. Slowly she opened her eyes and stared into the kindest emerald eyes framed by long dark lashes. Concern reflected from their depths, and she realized his strong arms were wrapped around her. A strange sense of comfort settled over her like a security blanket. For the first time in two days she felt sheltered and safe.

"Don't move," he cautioned. "The sheriff is trying to reach Doc Peters."

The gorgeous, truth-spinning lawyer held her. No! Not another lawyer.

The botched wedding, the bus trip, the last forty-eight

hours rushed back, the memories weaving icy tendrils of panic through her blood. This attorney probably knew her father's firm. This attorney could send her home, back to the drama she'd escaped.

"I'm fine," she blurted, sitting up straight and struggling out of his arms. "I don't need a doctor."

"Honey," the waitress soothed, bending down beside the lawyer, "no one has ever passed out in my restaurant. I think you best let the doctor examine you."

"No, I must have had low blood sugar or something," she said, making a motion to stand.

"It wouldn't hurt to let the doctor check you out," the handsome attorney said calmly. Why was it that attorneys never panicked? Never got excited. Why did people listen to and obey them?

Just like she'd believed and listened to Carter.

"I'm fine."

She stood, remembering with clarity that she had no money to pay the bill. No credit cards. No place to stay the night. She had nothing. And she refused to call her father.

She sank onto the chair at the table, needing a moment to think. Her trust held over a million dollars in funds, but a sudden withdrawal would bring the problems she'd run from racing to town.

"Okay, the excitement is over. Everyone back to their tables," Fran commanded, shooing everyone with her hands. "Girl, you sit right here. I'll get you a glass of water."

"Thanks," Valerie said, glancing down at her luggage. The two pieces sat right where she'd fallen beside them. She couldn't help but be a little suspicious of everyone after today.

"Hey, look. It's starting to snow outside," Fran called.

"Snow?"

"Yeah, we've got a big storm moving in tonight," the

handsome lawyer replied, standing beside the table, his emerald gaze studying her.

Oh no, where would she go? Deep breaths. She couldn't panic.

"We should have two feet of snow by morning," he said.

"Great," Valerie groaned.

"Where are you staying the night?" he asked.

"Um, the waitress mentioned the Springtown Inn. I'll probably be there."

His eyes raked her clothing. "You're not from around here are you?"

"No," she said quietly, wishing he would go away and leave her alone. Though his dark hair and gentle eyes were handsome enough to arouse even her bruised libido, his profession scared her worse than rattlesnakes.

She needed a quick spray of attorney repellant.

"Did you just get off the bus?" he asked, his voice deep and smooth.

"Yes."

"You're going to need a heavier coat than what you have on. Do you have one?"

God, the man was persistent with the questions. Why wouldn't he just leave?

"Yes," she lied, hoping he would get the hint.

"You're sure you don't need a doctor?" he asked. "It could be altitude sickness. Where did you come from?"

"Phoenix," she fibbed saying the first city that came to mind.

"No wonder you're dressed so lightly. The temperature is going to drop into the single digits tonight. You probably have a touch of altitude sickness. Take it easy the first few days you're here, and drink lots of water."

"Absolutely."

"What's your name?"

She swallowed, knowing she had to say something. But what? The police were probably searching for Valerie Burrows. "Valerie."

"Valerie…" he asked, gazing at her oddly. "Do you have a last name?" He looked at her suitcases. The monogram shined like a beacon. "DVB?"

"Valerie Brown," she muttered glancing over at his friend's brown uniform. She gave him her best trusting smile. Her heart thudded painfully in her chest, reminding her she was a terrible liar.

"Brown," he said sticking out his hand. "I'm Matt Jordan, and the sheriff is Jesse Phillips."

His grip was strong and his hands were warm. The pleasant woodsy fragrance of his cologne teased her senses.

"I'm sorry I've caused you so much trouble tonight."

Matt smiled. "It was nothing. Kind of nice to have a little excitement for a change. I'm just surprised it wasn't Fran's cooking that sent you over the edge."

"Hey, I heard that. You legal types can forget the free donuts and coffee."

The sheriff closed his cell phone and strolled to the table. "Doc Peters is unavailable. His nurse said to make sure you had plenty of fluids. She thinks it might be altitude sickness."

"Really, I'm feeling better," she lied. Fear pumped through her veins like an adrenaline junkie. She didn't need a doctor for what ailed her. She didn't need the sheriff to take her to jail. And she most definitely didn't need a lawyer to solve her problems. She needed a drama-free zone.

Matt nodded his head. "Ladies, the sheriff and I need to be going. Take it easy, Miss Brown."

"Thanks."

"Fran, if you need anything else, call me," the sheriff said. "Good night, Miss Brown."

"Night sheriff," Fran called.

Valerie watched the two men walk out the door of the café into the frosty night. The snow shimmied from the sky leaving a white sheen on the roads.

She had no cash, nothing, with a blizzard blowing outside. She was a trust fund baby, a well-bestowed one, though little good it did her now. How did she get herself out of this situation without calling her daddy for help?

Chapter Two

Thank God, the legal boys were gone. Now she could talk to Fran about the bill. She could ask about a homeless shelter or emergency housing for someone with no money.

How could she have sunk so low as to even consider a homeless shelter? She shivered at the thought.

A tiny voice reminded her she could always call her father. But a stronger one reminded her how he'd taken Carter's side and blamed her for her fiancé's indiscretion. The memory still hurt. She didn't need her father to solve her problems. The bus had dropped her in Springtown, and somehow she'd find a way to continue her journey away from her previous life.

The waitress hurried by, her arms loaded with plates. "Here you go, guys. Eat up. We're closing in thirty minutes, and you boys need to get on home before the roads become impassable."

"Fran, you sound more like my wife than a waitress," a male customer responded.

"No, Jim, if I was your wife, you would be home, serving me."

He laughed.

She swished by the table. "You need anything else, honey?"

Valerie took a deep breath, her pride in her throat. Never before had she been without money. "Yeah, can you sit with me for a moment?"

"Sure, sugar." The waitress sank onto the chair and gazed at Valerie. "You're in some kind of trouble, aren't you?"

"Well…"

"I knew it the moment you fainted. You're pregnant and running away from home."

Valerie wanted to smile, but her lips refused to move.

She was running away from a pregnancy, just not hers. "No."

"Your boyfriend is hunting you."

Almost. But more like her father and ex-fiancé, but that was too much information. "On the bus someone stole my wallet, and I didn't realize it until just a few minutes ago before I fainted."

"Oh, honey, I'm sorry."

"Yeah, well. It had all my money, my credit cards. I have no cash, nothing."

"Who can I call to help you?"

Valerie took a calming deep breath. No telephone calls. Plus her father still had access to all her accounts. She couldn't pull one penny without him knowing her whereabouts. Unless she wanted him and Carter to arrive in Springtown, she had to remain broke.

For the first time in her life, she was penniless, and the realization she was on her own hit home with startling clarity. Yes, she was a twenty-two-year-old pampered trust-fund baby released into the world like a newborn chick without a clue how to survive.

"No one."

"Sweetie, sometimes we get ourselves in predicaments where we have to swallow our pride and call someone to help us. I think you're in that situation."

"No calls." She could hear her father scolding her about getting into trouble again. No, this time she would find her own way.

Valerie glanced at the door and saw the Help Wanted sign. Maybe that was the solution. Stay in this one-horse town, get a job, and work until she earned enough money to continue on her journey to Denver. How long could it take to earn enough money for a bus ticket?

Fran crossed her arms and stared at her. "Okay, what are you going to do? You can't spend the night out on the streets. I mean, I won't charge you for the meal, but it's snowing, and you've gotta have some place to stay."

"What about the Help Wanted sign on the door? I want that job."

The waitress frowned and raised her brows, sizing her up.

"Don't take offense, sweetie, but you look more like the type of person that hires people to wait on you."

Valerie sighed. "I need the job."

"I guess you do."

"So will you hire me?"

"You sure you know what you're getting into? I mean, being a waitress is not easy, and these boys delight in being cantankerous."

"I need the money."

"All right, you're hired. Be here at five in the morning and prepared to work until two tomorrow afternoon. If you last the day, I'll be surprised."

God, that sounded like forever, but Valerie wouldn't complain. At least this way she didn't have to call her father. "Thank you. I can do this."

"You ever been a waitress before?"

"No, but I'm a fast learner."

"I sure hope you know what you're doing."

Valerie shrugged. Her choices were limited, and her pride refused to make that phone call. "Is there a homeless shelter where I can spend the night?"

The waitress leaned back and chuckled aloud. "Honey, we don't have homeless here in our town. But I know of someone who's looking to rent a room out. Let me call and see if she's agreeable to taking you in."

~

Fran's car came to a halt in front of a two-story log home that belonged on the front of a Christmas card. Warm light reflected from the windows. Icicles hung from the eves, and smoke drifted from the rooftop. Valerie imagined a large family gathered in front of a crackling fire, drinking hot chocolate, laughing and enjoying one another. The kind of family she'd often dreamed of but never experienced.

Fran turned the car off, drawing Valerie's attention to her. "Now, before I introduce you to McKenzie Palmer, there are some things you need to know."

Foreboding trickled like a river fall through Valerie, and her overloaded sense of protection went on high alert.

"McKenzie's husband died a year ago of a brain tumor. They diagnosed it, and before they had much time to say good-bye, he was gone. McKenzie's still learning to cope with the loss of her husband. Not to mention being a single parent with twins."

"That's terrible."

"Yeah, well, the worst part is he didn't have much insurance, and it's a struggle to keep the house and take care of their twins. So that's why she needs a boarder."

"She's never done this before?"

"Nope. And I trust you not to steal her blind."

"I have no need to steal…" Valerie stopped. Money was no longer just an ATM transaction away. Money she no longer had access to. Money she'd never done without. Broke, flat broke, and unless she wanted to crawl back to her father, she would remain broke. "I don't steal."

Fran smiled. "Good." She opened the car door and hurried to the back where Valerie's suitcases were stored. "Come on, this ain't the Hilton and I'm not your bellhop."

Valerie opened the car door and stepped outside. The icy wind tore right through her thin jacket to settle into her bones. What had possessed her to come to Colorado in winter without a coat? Her suitcase was packed with her new Caribbean honeymoon wardrobe. The three bikinis she'd packed were as useless as a parka in the Sahara.

Fran handed her one of the two suitcases, and Valerie carried her luggage through several inches of snow.

Gingerly, they made their way through the wet white wet ice particles and clambered up the wooden porch. While they were kicking the snow off their shoes, the door burst open, and a beautiful young blond woman with two blue-eyed twin toddlers wrapped around her legs.

"Hi, Fran," she said, as she stared at Valerie.

Sad brown eyes stared at Valerie, and for a moment she forgot about the misadventure that had landed her in Colorado. Raw pain reflected from the young woman's gaze.

Valerie held out her hand. "I'm Valerie Brown."

"McKenzie Palmer," she replied, taking her hand. "And these are my twins, Austin and Ashley."

"Hello." Valerie smiled at the children. They gazed at her with a curious expression.

McKenzie held open the door. "Come in where it's warm."

The two women carried in the suitcases and dropped them to the floor.

"Fran said you would rent me a room for one hundred dollars a week?" Valerie asked.

"Yes, plus any long distance charges on the phone."

"Okay."

"You're awfully young," the woman said, her gaze questioning. "Just so you know, I don't allow any men in the room."

"I don't know anyone in town, so that's not a problem."

"Good. Follow me and I'll show you where you'll be staying."

The three women and two children climbed the stairs to a bedroom situated at the rear of the house. McKenzie led her into a soft yellow room with flowered wallpaper. A small bathroom was tucked into the eaves of the house.

"Nice," Valerie commented, thinking that her room at home was twice this big with a Jacuzzi tub and separate shower. But that was a former life, and she was determined to live on her own terms, at least until the fiasco of her doomed wedding faded from the spotlight. A spotlight she'd never enjoyed.

"My mother-in-law used this room," McKenzie said. "Six months ago she remarried and has her own home now."

"Oh."

"Girls, I hate to break up this tea party, but I got to get home and rest. Four o'clock comes awfully early." Fran gave McKenzie a hug. "Things are going to be fine."

"Yes, they are."

"Missy, I will pick you up at four thirty sharp. Don't make me honk the horn or pound on the door. Be ready and waiting."

Panic seized Valerie as the one person who'd helped her was about to walk out the door and leave her alone. This all seemed so very strange. She swallowed to keep the panic at bay. "Thanks, Fran. How should I dress?"

The older woman chuckled. "Wear something you don't mind getting stained. Food just seems to have a way of jumping onto your clothes during the day."

McKenzie stood at the door to the bedroom. "I'll see Fran to the door while you unpack. You can use the chest to put your belongings in, or the closet."

"Thanks." Valerie stopped for a moment and remembered, she didn't have a cell phone. "Do you offer a wake-up call in the morning, or is there a service I can use?"

Fran burst out laughing. "Yeah, it's called an alarm clock. Set it correctly."

McKenzie shifted from the door to face Valerie, a small smile on her lips. "I have a spare one you can use."

"Thanks." Valerie realized with startling clarity that there were so many things about her old life that she took for granted.

~

Valerie would never be rude to another waitress again for the rest of her life. Her feet and arms ached. Her mouth felt tight from smiling, and she reeked of greasy fried foods. She felt like a smiling, soggy, french fry.

"Honey, table one is waving at you. They need something," Fran prompted, a coffee pot dangling from her hand.

"A good lesson in manners," Valerie grumbled, thinking she'd never worked harder for so little money. No wonder Fran thought she'd quit before the end of the day. But the image of Carter's car kept her feet moving.

"They need a smile and more coffee. Watch and learn."

Fran grinned brightly as she approached the table. "You boys need a refill?"

"Fran, my eggs are not cooked enough, and my bacon is tough."

He needed some cheese to go with that whine or maybe even a waa-ambulance.

Valerie observed Fran frown at the older man who had complained nonstop since she'd waited on their table. He looked like Santa Claus with horns, only he'd lost his way back to the North Pole. She'd gladly find him directions if it would send him on his way.

"Now, Charlie," Fran said gently, "if you've got a gripe with the cook, you need to talk to Todd." She filled the coffee cups at the table. "You've been coming here long enough to know that, so why are you harassing my new girl?"

"Ah, Fran, we're just trying to break her in right."

"Well, if you don't stop your whining, the next time

you come in your eggs will have a new spice sprinkled on them. Arsenic."

He laughed good-naturedly. "You wouldn't do that."

She raised her brows. "If you run off my help, I may just go a little postal, and I won't be responsible for my actions. Now, do you boys need anything else? Do you want me to return your eggs to the cook?"

"My eggs are fine. I just wanted to rile that cute little miss."

"Be nice, Charlie." She whirled around and strode directly to Valerie.

"They're just a bunch of good ole boys who know you're new in town. Don't let them get away with anything. Always turn the complaint back on them in a good-natured way. They just want someone to make them feel important."

"Thanks Fran," Valerie said.

"Don't worry, honey. Soon they'll find someone else to pick on. If not, come get me, and I'll make the curve in the crack of their backsides jagged."

So far this job had made Valerie feel even more disjointed than the rest of her life. Yet, in less than a minute Fran had managed to disarm the situation. She could charm the socks off a terrorist and sweet talk him into jail. A lesson Valerie desperately needed. "Thanks, Fran."

"Hang in there, kid. You're doing okay. Being a waitress ain't the easiest job in the world."

A surge of pride gave Valerie a boost of much-needed energy. Fran said she was doing a good job! Other than the temp job in her father's law practice, this was her first real employment. And her father liked to regale his cronies with stories of her screw-ups in the office.

The bell above the door dinged, announcing a new customer. Valerie turned, ready to seat the latest arrival. She stopped in her food-stained sneakers at the sight of the one person in town she could have gone all day without seeing. Attorney Matt Jordan.

Her lawyer magnet clicked on and a tingle of awareness danced along her spine. No! With only seventy-two hours since her last relationship disaster, she mentally switched off the magnet. No more men. No more lawyers.

Still, he could have graced the cover of *GQ* or *The American Lawyer*.

Her heart danced a little mambo when he smiled at her and seated himself. Why couldn't he be some ugly, slimy nerd she could easily ignore?

She strolled over to him. "What can I get you, Mr. Jordan?"

His green eyes reflected surprise, and her radar went on high alert. "Aren't you the girl who fainted last night?"

"Yeah," she acknowledged, her order pad in hand, he would just tell her what he wanted and forget the small talk.

"You feel better?"

"Much."

"So why are you here? Last night you seemed determined to rent a car and drive to Denver. What made you decide to stay in town?" he asked casually.

He'd overheard her say she intended to rent a car? She didn't know how to respond. Her pride refused to publicly acknowledge her financial situation. With only ten dollars in tips to her name, it was difficult to discuss money.

"I decided to try the small-town life for a while."

He grinned. "Why would a big-city girl like you decide Springtown was someplace you wanted to stay? And being a waitress? You don't seem the type."

Sometimes it was hard to resist the urge to answer stupid questions with an equally dim-witted response. So she didn't.

"It's my first stop as Miss America. I'm here to

promote world peace."

He stared at her as if she'd lost her mind, and then he laughed. "I guess that means it's none of my business. I'll take coffee."

"Cream or sugar?"

"Just black." He glanced at her shoes. "At least you traded in your heels for something a little more sensible."

She lowered her order pad and looked down at the sneakers she had on. "Yeah, I didn't want to stain my heels with food. My Jimmy Choo's would not have lasted the first hour."

"I have a shoe-aholic sister."

"Really. Your sister likes shoes? I need to meet this woman."

Valerie heard her rowdy table calling her and wanted to flip them the finger, but she wanted to eat more. "What can I get you, Mr. Jordan? I've got to wait on my other table."

The attorney gave the other table a stern gaze. "Charlie, give the girl a minute to take my order."

"You've had her for more than a minute already," the man taunted.

Matt grinned. "I can't help it if she's attracted to my charm."

Valerie shook her head. If she didn't need the job, she would have told them both to kiss off. She was immune to Matt Jordan's charms. He was a man. An arrogant lawyer. She didn't need the aggravation and refused to respond to the comments from either table.

In a firm voice she asked, "I have your drink order. What else?"

Matt gave her his order and then watched as she hurried to the kitchen counter. She picked up the coffee pot, went to the table of rambunctious forestry workers, filled their cups, and smiled. They melted under the voltage of her curved lips. Her smile packed a thousand watts of pure charm, and every man at that table was affected.

What was this girl doing in Springtown? He could see her in Los Angeles or New York, but not a small mountain village on the edge of the Rockies.

She moved through the restaurant, the label on her snug Yanuk jeans that hugged her hips and legs riding low on her waist. There was a classiness about her that seemed out of place in a small town café. An air of worldliness and wealth that he guessed no university could teach.

And Yanuk jeans were not cheap.

So, why had she decided to stay? And why had she arrived on the bus? She appeared more the BMW convertible type than someone who used public transportation.

Fran stopped at his table. "Why aren't you in the big city defending some criminal?"

"I'm not a criminal lawyer. And I don't have to travel to Denver until next week," Matt responded.

"Well, aren't I just lucky that you came by then?"

"Yep, I see your rot-gut food didn't kill our out-of-town guest." He watched Valerie carrying plates of food. "So what made you decide to hire her?"

"I needed a waitress and she needed a job. Simple case of supply and demand."

"She doesn't look like the kind of woman who works as a waitress," he commented, staring as she moved efficiently through the restaurant, her arms loaded with dirty dishes.

"Even city girls have to eat."

"I thought she was headed out of town," he asked, trying to understand what had happened between the time Valerie fainted and when he left the café.

"She changed her mind," Fran responded. "A woman has that right."

"It just seems odd. She gets off the bus, faints, and now

she's working in your café."

"Leave it alone, Jordan. I've got a new employee."

Matt couldn't get enough of the young woman. God, she was nice to look at. Her full lips and high cheekbones were model worthy. His gaze swept down past her neck to her high breasts, and a stirring he'd ignored for the past year sprang to life.

"Matthew Jordan, don't ogle my hired help. It's not polite," Fran reminded him.

He smiled at the lady he'd grown fond of. "It may not be polite, but she's a damn pretty sight."

"That she is, and I'm a mite protective of her. She doesn't seem to have anyone looking after her." Fran crossed her arms over her chest and stared down at him. "Back off. I think she's a little fragile right now."

"If that's fragile, I'd hate to see her at full strength."

"Some people can hide their emotions well."

"What makes you think she's fragile?" he questioned, wondering if that was the reason she'd fainted.

"Woman's intuition, I guess. She almost seems afraid."

He gazed at the young woman carrying a plate to a customer and sighed. "I can only handle one emotional woman at a time."

"Speaking of McKenzie, have you spoken to her today?"

"Briefly. Austin's sick. I'm on my way over there to stay with Ashley while McKenzie takes Austin to the doctor."

"Did she tell you about—"

"Fran, I need you in the kitchen!" the cook yelled from the back.

The waitress dropped her arms and spun towards the kitchen. "Gotta run."

As Fran hurried away, Matt watched the new pretty waitress. Valerie Brown's looks had his male hormones spiking his libido into overdrive. Yesterday in his arms she'd felt soft and vulnerable. Yet today she appeared determined to tackle the world and any hungry customer who ventured in the Mountain Chalet Café.

Why Fran thought Valerie was fragile, he didn't know, but he didn't have the time to investigate. The welfare of his sister, niece, and nephew were his top priority.

Chapter Three

Matt opened the door to his sister's house, and Mrs. Graham, her neighbor, held a finger to her mouth. "Ashley's asleep in the playpen."

"Where's McKenzie?"

"The doctor's office called and said they had a cancellation, so she left earlier than expected."

"She should have called me. I could have come immediately."

The elderly woman smiled. "I was here when they called, so I told her I would stay with Ashley until you arrived. It's been less than an hour ago. I expect her back anytime now."

"Thanks, Mrs. Graham, I can take it from here."

"Yes, I should be going. If you need me, I'm right across the road."

"Be careful walking home."

"Bye, dear."

Matt watched her leave and then sank down into a chair. He hated just sitting. He checked Ashley, who lay curled on her side, sleeping, unaware that her Mommy had left.

Every time one of the kids got the sniffles, Matt worried. What if Austin was coming down with something serious? He'd promised his brother-in-law, John, he would protect McKenzie and their family. And though his promise seemed easy at the time of John's death, Matt worried about McKenzie and the children.

His sister was a strong, vibrant, tough woman. But sometimes the sadness etched on her face left him aching for her. She missed John.

In the few short years they were married, John had made McKenzie happy, and for the first time since their parents' messy divorce, Matt began to believe in marriage once again.

Watching the love between John and McKenzie had made him realize the depths of his own loneliness and for the first time reconsider bachelorhood.

Now when he was ready to experience for himself a loving relationship, it wasn't forthcoming. There wasn't even a blip on his radar of finding someone to share his life with. He had the time, the money, and he hoped the skills needed to provide his wife a good home. But no matter how much he searched for the perfect woman, she was as elusive as an insurance company admitting guilt.

Unable to sit any longer, he tucked the blanket around Ashley and ran his hand over her smooth skin. She looked so sweet and innocent, and he loved both of the twins more than he thought possible. He grabbed the baby monitor. He'd feed the horses and make sure they had plenty of water while Ashley slept. If she awoke, he could hear her on the radio.

Safely tucked in her crib, Ashley would be all right until he returned.

~

After a long day at the café, Valerie wanted nothing more than to return to the house, peel off her clothes, and crawl into bed. She had a new appreciation for working women and longed to soak in a hot tub. But before she could reach the door, the sound of a child's cries echoed from the house.

She swung open the back door and ran through the mudroom only to find Ashley standing in the playpen, tears streaming down her cheeks. Her cries were loud enough to wake the dead two counties over. Valerie hurried to the crib. Why hadn't McKenzie responded to the child's tears?

"Hey, sweetheart, what's wrong?" she asked as Ashley sobbed. No one responded to Valerie's voice, and Ashley continued to exercise her lungs.

Why is the baby alone?

"McKenzie?"

Silence greeted her. Valerie reached into the playpen to pick Ashley up to comfort her and encountered one of the child's problems. The toddler was soaked.

"Baby, I'd cry, too. Come on, I'll change you, and we'll go find your mommy."

She lifted Ashley out of the crib and carried the baby upstairs to the nursery, where she placed her on the changing table. Though she'd never been around children much, she knew enough to change a diaper. The toddler's cries slowed, though small hiccups emitted from her.

"Momma?" she asked.

"We'll find her," Valerie promised, trying to soothe Ashley's fears. One wrong move and the child's lungs and Valerie's ears would get another workout.

Quickly, she removed the soaked diaper, swiped Ashley with a wipe, powdered her, and put on a fresh diaper. Curiosity darkened the depths of the baby's big blue eyes.

"Now you're all set. Let's go find your mommy. She can't be far."

The back door opened, and a loud male voice cursed. "Ashley!"

Valerie stepped to the nursery door at the top of the stairs to see Matt frantically searching the living room. "Mr. Jordan?"

He gazed up at her, an odd expression on his face. "What are you doing with Ashley?"

Valerie walked down the stairs. "She was crying, so I changed her."

Ashley held out her arms to him, and he took the baby from Valerie. "What are *you* doing here?"

"Maybe I should ask you the same question. What are

you doing here?" she asked, trying to keep the defensive tone from her voice. She was dead-dog tired, and here was the one man she wanted to avoid at all costs.

"This is my sister's home and I'm babysitting."

"McKenzie is your sister?" she asked, shocked.

"Yes."

"And you left your niece alone?"

"I was gone five minutes to the barn to feed McKenzie's horses and make sure everything was okay while Ashley slept. I took the baby monitor."

"Did you turn it on?" she questioned, her voice stern.

He glanced at the monitor in his hands. "Ah, let me see." He hit the switch and they could hear the sound of their breathing on the device in his hand.

"It's useless without power," Valerie said, her voice echoing in the radio.

"Well, I meant to," he responded, his gaze flickering to the child. "Why are you here?"

Valerie gazed at the big man holding Ashley and bouncing the child in his arms.

"McKenzie didn't tell you?" Valerie asked.

"Tell me what?"

"I'm her new roommate."

His forehead creased in a frown, and his brows drew together. For a moment he didn't say anything. "She would have told me if she had let you move in."

"It was late last night."

"She would have said something today."

"Well, where is she? Why don't you ask her why she didn't tell you I was living with her now.

"She had to take Austin to the doctor."

"Obviously, she had more important things on her mind than telling you I had moved in."

He glanced at her empty hands. "How long have you been here?"

"Long enough to change the baby's diaper and steal McKenzie's jewels," Valerie all but snapped.

"I didn't accuse you."

"You didn't have to. I could see what you were thinking. The trashy waitress is going to steal your sister blind." She clenched her jaw to hold back the retort she so wanted to fling at him. She had enough money in her trust fund to take care of anything she needed. But he'd never believe her. "You're holding her most prized possession!"

"That's not what I was thinking! I was concerned about my niece," he said, his voice rising.

"Check out the guest room. You'll find I've moved in." Valerie was too tired. Her feet hurt, her back ached, and she felt numb from the week's events. Her nerves were stretched, screaming for release, and another lawyer was giving her crap. Screaming might just be the release she needed if he didn't back off.

"Again, I didn't say anything about you stealing. You're the one who brought up the subject. It surprised me to find a stranger in McKenzie's home holding her child."

Valerie strode to Matt and poked him in the chest with her finger. "No one should go off and leave a baby alone, even when she's asleep. You should be a little more responsible."

"I...I was gone for five minutes," he said defensively. "I went to the barn to take care of her horses. I was trying to help."

"Well, in less than five minutes Ashley woke up and was crying. What if the house had caught on fire?"

For a moment he stared at her as if she were a green goblin. Ashley pushed against his chest, wanting down. He set her on the floor, and when he stood, Valerie could see the wheels in his brain turning from the expression on his face.

"Wait a minute. You've switched the conversation.

You tell me you're living here, yet McKenzie hasn't confirmed that information. I don't know who the hell you are."

"Watch your language, Mr. Hotshot Attorney. There's a child present," Valerie said quietly, her voice calm.

All attorneys should be loaded into a boat and dumped in the ocean. They were all jerks! Even her father, and most especially Carter.

Ashley stared at the adults, her face screwed up, and she began to wail.

"Now you've done it. You made her cry," Valerie said. She leaned down and picked the child up and sank into a nearby rocker, where she soothed the toddler.

"There, there, baby, it's okay," she said patting her back.

Matt opened his mouth to speak but only stared at her, frustration evident in his posture. God, it felt good to make an attorney speechless. Even if he was the wrong one.

A car pulled into the driveway and saved her from his response. "McKenzie's here, and she can confirm that I now occupy the upstairs bedroom her mother-in-law once occupied. Should I tell her how you left Ashley alone?"

"No! Don't give her anything else to worry about. She's got enough to deal with," he said, his voice stern.

Well, she'd certainly found a subject the lawyer was touchy about. Ashley snuggled in close as Valerie rocked her, her sweet baby smell oddly soothing.

McKenzie struggled through the door, her arms loaded with a sleeping Austin. She glanced around the room. "Hi. I see you two have met."

Ashley squealed with delight at the sight of her mother. She hoped off Valerie's lap to run to McKenzie. "Just a minute, baby. Let me get your brother in bed. Go see Uncle Matt."

The little girl glanced at her uncle and proceeded to

climb onto Valerie's lap.

"Hey, I'm the uncle," he exclaimed to Ashley, who turned and buried her head against Valerie's chest, ignoring him.

McKenzie hurried up the stairs with Austin.

Matt moved across the room and rested his arm against the fireplace mantel, tension evident in the way he stood. Valerie ignored him as she rocked and crooned to Ashley. A grandfather clock ticked the seconds like a time bomb echoing in the room. A time bomb with Valerie as the fuse.

Ten minutes later a tired, worried-looking McKenzie came downstairs, obviously not needing a confrontation.

"Anyone want a cup of tea?" she asked, walking into the kitchen, where she filled a kettle with water.

"No. How's Austin?" Matt asked, his voice sharp.

"He has an ear infection. But the doctor said we caught it early."

"Poor little guy," Matt replied. "How can I help you?"

McKenzie glanced between the two of them, sensing the obvious strain. "Staying with Ashley was a huge relief. She would have been a handful in the waiting room."

He tilted his head toward Valerie, and his forehead drew into a frown. "Did you rent a bedroom to her?"

"Yes," she responded nonchalantly as she placed the kettle on the stove.

Matt strode over to his sister and said quietly, "I told you I would help you. If you need money, let me know."

McKenzie sighed and gazed at her brother. "Thank you for the offer, but I can't spend the rest of my life depending on you."

Appearing to dismiss him, she turned to the cabinet and pulled out cups and bags of tea.

"But you know nothing about her. You could be putting yourself or the kids in danger," he said, his voice barely a whisper.

"This is why I hadn't told you," McKenzie said.

Valerie wanted to throw something at the attorney. She snapped, "Yeah, I'm definitely the criminal type. I wear Jimmy Choo shoes, have a Rolex watch, used to drive a Corvette—"

He whirled around to face Valerie, frustration evident on his handsome face. "You said the key phrase there. Used to. So what happened? Too much cocaine, or did you spend all of Daddy's money and now you're on the run?"

Valerie bit back the response she wanted to shout at him. For the first time in her life, words slapped her with the truth. Oh, she'd never done drugs, but Daddy's money had always supported her. And now she was on the run, but that didn't make her a criminal did it? Well…technically…

"Look, your sister needs help, and I needed a place to stay. We worked out a deal. I could never hurt or harm anyone intentionally."

Yet she had hurt her fiancé or at least his prized possession. But he'd deserved what she'd done. Now…well, maybe it hadn't been her most rational moment. A simple case of temporary insanity brought on by extreme emotional distress. A simple case of temporary insanity brought on by a cheating groom and her best friend.

Matt stared at her as if he were looking deep in her soul, and while normally she would have met his gaze head-on, she somehow felt a little ashamed of her actions. She didn't regret them, but most definitely she'd missed the high road and taken the revenge bypass. Sooner or later she would have to confront her actions, but not yet. She needed time to gain some perspective and to let her wounds heal before dealing with Carter.

"Matt, we'll be fine. You have no reason to worry," McKenzie said to her brother. "You've helped me more in the last year than any sister has the right to expect."

He ignored McKenzie, his eyes riveted on Valerie. "Tell me why you decided to stay in Springtown when I overheard you say in the café last night that you were headed to Denver."

She returned his stare. "Simple. Snow. Last night you said it yourself—the weather was going to get bad. It did and I stayed."

"It's okay, Matt," McKenzie repeated to her brother, this time a little stronger.

"The storm has passed, and yet here you are working in the café. Why?"

"The storm passed and I liked this town so much I decided to just hang out for a while."

His emerald gaze pierced her for a few moments, silently contemplating her. Giving her probably one of his best lawyer faces, only he didn't realize she was immune to the authoritative expressions. Immune to the prosecution and the defense manipulation of her emotions. They no longer fazed her, as she'd grown up with them.

"You're lying. I don't know why, but I'm not buying your answers."

"Maybe. Maybe not," she admitted, refusing to back down, not offering any additional information. It was none of his business, and indifference had always driven her daddy crazy.

His emerald eyes sparkled in the silent test of wills.

McKenzie walked over and laid her hand on her brother's arm. "Matt, Valerie is not going to hurt us. I'm letting her stay."

He turned on his sister, his voice clipped. "If you want a stranger staying in your home at least draw up a lease. I can print one off and bring it by."

"A lease isn't necessary. Valerie doesn't know how long she'll be here, so we're taking it one day at a time," she assured him.

With a sigh, he turned his gaze to Valerie. "For now, I have no choice but to let this go. I don't condone liars. In fact, I detest liars with a passion. If one hair is harmed on my family, anything, your new accommodations will be the Springtown jail. Your Jimmy Choo shoes won't look too good with an orange jumpsuit."

Her father had every employee's background verified. Matt could do the same. Valerie felt certain he would use his connections to do a background check on Valerie Brown. Just how long she had before he came back and started asking more questions, she didn't know, but for tonight she would still sleep under a roof.

She shouldn't have goaded him quite so much, but somehow he represented every stinking lawyer in her life, and since the people who hurt her weren't there to express her anger to, he was a good substitute. A substitute who might not have deserved her frustration, but one she'd enjoyed sparring with just the same.

"Sorry, Matt," she said sarcastically. "I'm sure the accommodations at the Springtown jail are not up to my standards. McKenzie and I will be just fine. Now don't you have some briefs or something that need writing? Your sister and I have some serious shoe talk to get to."

Chapter Four

Valerie watched as Matt's green eyes darkened with anger. His mouth had a determined set, yet he pivoted on his heel and retreated without saying a word. For a moment Valerie feared she'd said too much, but when she glanced over at McKenzie, the woman was smiling.

The door slammed shut as Matt made his exit. The two roommates looked at one another and burst out laughing.

"No one has ever gotten to my stubborn brother like that before. That was priceless." She sighed. "Matt means well, but since John died, he's suffocated me with his protection."

Valerie sank onto an overstuffed chair that faced McKenzie. "Don't apologize for Matt. It's really sweet that he's watching out for you."

"Yes, it is. I'm lucky to have him."

Ashley crawled onto McKenzie's lap and snuggled against her mother. An odd sensation warmed Valerie's chest as she realized this child would never know her father. For just a moment, she missed her own dad, but then she remembered how he'd taken Carter's side. No, she refused to think about Carter or her father for a while. She needed a mental break from the pain of their betrayal.

"I meant what I said. I would never intentionally harm you or the children." She paused, her fists clenching to restrain the pain, wondering how much she should tell McKenzie. "My life is in shambles right now. I need somewhere to stay until I make some decisions. I could be here a week or maybe six months. I don't know."

McKenzie nodded. "I appreciate your honesty. But you wouldn't be here if I was the least bit concerned. My brother will come around. Eventually he'll realize that I'm not going to accept his financial help and he's not going to dictate how I live my life." She sighed. "John's death really affected him. I think he's realized his own mortality. For the first time, he's talking kids and marriage. After our parents' divorce, he swore he would never marry."

She gazed at Valerie. "How about you?" she teased. "You certainly aren't afraid to take on "The Crusher."

"The Crusher?" A chill went down Valerie's spine. She'd heard the name mentioned in her father's law office.

"Yeah, Matt's won more legal liability cases than anyone else in the state. He's known as the Colorado Crusher."

Valerie's insides twisted into a knot and her breath caught. Of all the towns where she could have gotten off that bus, she had to stop in the city where Colorado's most successful liability lawyer lived. She knew from her father that Matt was not some private, two or three cases a year attorney. He was known for his toughness and his ability to sway a jury. His reputation was to crush the opposition and win.

And to make things worse, he wanted to get married. The urge to run was almost overwhelming. She didn't want to be around anyone determined to be married. She didn't want to be around another successful attorney. She didn't want to be around a man with a smile that was tempting. Not now.

"Well, I'm taking a sabbatical from men right now." She wanted McKenzie to know up front that she was not interested in being involved with anyone.

But most especially lawyers.

Something in her voice must have given her away, as McKenzie stopped running her fingers through her daughter's hair and studied her closely.

"Is that why you came to Springtown? To get away from a man?" McKenzie asked.

Valerie genuinely liked McKenzie, but she couldn't respond. In the last few days she'd managed to shore up the dam that held the reservoir of her feelings for her disastrous wedding. She wasn't ready to let that river flow again. Not yet. "Right now, I need to stay focused on me."

"He must have hurt you pretty bad."

Valerie sat there, surprised. "Who?"

"The man you're running from."

Great! She didn't need anyone speculating about her and a man, even if it was true. This conversation was at an end.

"Show me the shoes you have. I'd really like to see them."

McKenzie smiled knowingly and stood. "Come on. I'll even let you try them on if they fit."

~

Matt stared at the blinking cursor, anger smoldering within. A stack of paperwork piled in front of him, the phone rang constantly, the fax ran 24/7, and he wished a magic fairy would appear and do the filing.

The blinking cursor's image took shape in his mind. Five feet ten inches with sapphire eyes and a smart mouth. Tonight his mind refused to focus on his job. Instead, he obsessed on the blonde beauty that had practically kicked him out of his sister's house. The woman who'd stepped off a bus, created a scene by fainting, and then never left. The woman he felt both attracted to and repelled by.

The woman had nerve. She waltzed into town, charmed Fran into giving her a job, and cast a spell over McKenzie, who let her move in.

Valerie Brown was a very determined, beautiful woman who could charm a snake handler.

Well, she didn't intimidate him. He'd just do a little research to find out what kind of person she was and maybe in the process learn why she remained in Springtown, Colorado. No one came to the small town by chance and decided to stay. After all, industry was nil and job prospects were few.

At first Matt had remained here only because of McKenzie and his niece and nephew.

In the beginning he'd resented the fact that McKenzie wouldn't move back to Denver. No matter how much he pleaded with her, she refused to give up the home she'd built with her late husband. McKenzie insisted her children would be reared in a small town, and until the day her bank account ran dry, she refused to move. Often McKenzie reminded him this was her life, not his, and he was free to go.

But he couldn't leave. And he didn't want to go. After his promise to John, Matt felt obligated to stay and help her with the twins. Six months passed, and the town had grown on him. Sure he missed fancy dining, Broncos games, and concerts, but something about the orange glow of the setting sun against the Rockies, the fresh pine scent, and the lack of traffic jams had a way of easing the tension from his bones. And nothing compared to the whisper of the Aspens rustling through an open window.

He loved the area so much he bought five acres close to McKenzie's property and was building his own log home.

The only thing missing was someone to decorate the house and sit on the covered porch with him in the evening. He wanted a wife, someone to be the mother of his children.

Before the move, his job had kept him so busy that he hadn't had time for a relationship, but now that he worked at a slower pace, he'd had time to notice his loneliness.

The romantic pickings in Springtown were slim, or so he believed. Certainly, Valerie Brown's pert breasts, long legs, and curvaceous hips caught and held his interest. But he needed more than just breasts to keep him interested in a woman. He needed a quick mind to challenge him and a woman his children would be proud to call Mother.

Valerie Brown was a mystery woman. A woman he knew nothing about except that she had expensive clothes, no money, and apparently had moved in with his sister.

He wasn't a snob. Though Cinderella's chariot was strictly coach, her makeup, manicure, and haircut spoke of high-dollar salons. How could he be attracted and yet wary at the same time? Valerie was different from the women he found himself normally attracted to. She was mouthier and more demanding. But the bus thing bothered him the most. Why didn't she have a car?

Unable to stop himself, he went to Google and searched Valerie Brown. A beautiful African American singer's picture popped up. Not the right Valerie Brown. A list blinked onto the monitor. A woman supervisor in Los Angeles County, a married woman, and then a doctor, but none were the Valerie Brown living in his sister's home.

He went to Facebook and did a random search. Several Valerie's were listed, but none that had long blonde hair or sparkling blue eyes. Not one had ripe lips full of attitude that begged to be kissed.

So he'd found nothing on the spunky waitress.

Still, he could ask Jesse to run a background check on the mysterious Valerie. He paused for a moment. Was he overreacting? The image of his niece snuggled trustfully against the woman's breast came to mind, and he realized the stakes were way too high.

He'd do anything to protect his sister and her children, even if it meant prying into the life of the mysterious transient woman who made his pulse quicken.

Who was he kidding? He wanted to know who Valerie Brown was.

~

The next day Matt slid into the booth at the café where

he met Jesse at least two or three times a week. He'd called and told his friend to meet him for lunch. Valerie hadn't seen him when he walked in, so he had seated himself.

He watched Jesse stroll in, and Valerie waved to him with her free hand.

"Go ahead and take a seat. I'll be right there to get your drink order," she called.

"Sure, Valerie," Jesse said. "I'm going to join Matt."

She froze and slowly her head turned to glance over her shoulder at him. Her brows drew together in a frown, and she lowered them in obvious disapproval before she returned to her customers.

He gazed at her as she poured coffee, handed out menus, and talked casually with a group of forestry workers. Her blue jeans fit snug across her shapely rear, and her short-cropped sweater occasionally gave a glimpse of her smooth skin. He took a deep breath and tried to still his racing pulse.

What was it about this girl that made him want to stare like a college kid? What about her attracted him and repelled him at the same time? It would be a miracle if she had a high school education. Yet something about her had him wanting to throw her over his shoulder and walk out the door. He'd kiss her until she told him what he wanted to know.

Only then would he feel safe with her staying at his sister's home.

"Fran's new waitress definitely gives an air of improvement to this place, doesn't she?" Jesse commented as he slid into the booth across from him.

Matt jerked his attention to his friend. "Hi."

"Now you notice me."

"Shut up!" Matt said, half-teasing, half-serious. "I saw you walk in the door. I was counting the number of boys from the forestry service that seem to have time for lunch these days."

"You are busted, my friend. You were checking out the fit of her jeans," Jesse said, scanning the specials scrawled on a chalkboard at the front of the cafe.

"Come on," Matt said good-naturedly, knowing he'd been caught.

"Fran's business is seeing a lot more male customers since Valerie came to work for her," Jesse commented without glancing up from the menu. "Just look around."

The café did seem to have more customers. The biggest percentage of them worked for the county road department.

"Most of these guys are married," Matt declared, trying to contain his annoyance, knowing he'd enjoyed every second of watching the way she moved.

How was it possible she both infuriated him and attracted him at the same time?

"Never hurts to look."

"We don't know anything about this girl."

"Do you really think these guys want to sit down and have a conversation with her?" Jesse said, glancing from his menu to laugh at his friend.

"No," Matt replied, strangely angry. "So they came here to gawk at her?"

"Pretty, new girl in town. She's a novelty."

"That's what concerns me," Matt acknowledged.

"Why? Why are you acting so strange about this girl? Just because she came from the big city, doesn't mean she's a criminal," Jesse pointed out.

"In case you haven't heard, she's moved in with McKenzie," Matt hissed with frustration. "My sister has gone through enough. She doesn't need some girl robbing her blind."

Jesse frowned at Matt and turned his gaze upon Valerie. When he glanced back at Matt, there was a teasing glint in his eyes. "I don't normally arrest people because they look suspicious and arrive in town on the bus. I think she's okay."

Matt leaned closer to Jesse. "Spoken like a small-town sheriff who's not read about the woman who came home to find her house and bank account cleaned out by her roommate."

Jesse shook his head. "McKenzie has a good head on her shoulders. I don't think she would have let Valerie move in if she thought there could be a problem."

"How would she know? Valerie's been in town forty-eight hours. There was no background check or even a lease signed."

"Spoken like a lawyer. People do still help one another without formal leases."

Jesse cleared his throat loudly and nudged him beneath the table.

"What do we know about this girl," Matt exclaimed trying to curtail the frustrated tone of his voice, not understanding Jesse's signal until it was too late.

"We know she's five feet ten inches, weighs approximately one hundred and twenty pounds of trouble, and she's standing right behind you. Good afternoon, gentlemen," Valerie said. "Could I interest you in the special of the day? Beef stew with homemade cornbread and a slice of banana cream pie?"

Jesse laughed nervously. "You are so busted, man."

Her voice was too nice. She'd heard him.

"Busted as in, yes, I heard everything," she said icily.

Jesse closed the menu. "I'll take the special."

"And for you, Mr. Jordan?" She asked, her voice too polite. "How about a serving of humble pie? I'm sure I can convince Todd to fix some for you."

Her comment stunned him for about thirty seconds. Her sapphire eyes glistened with irritation.

"I don't see humble pie on the menu," he challenged,

surprised at her spunk. He knew she was still angry with him from last night, and today she'd overheard him.

"It's reserved for *special* customers like you."

Jesse started to snicker and Matt glared at him.

"And why am I considered special?" he asked.

She smiled and put one hand on her hip as her eyes went wide and innocent. "Well, honey, it's a proven fact that all lawyers think they're *special*."

"I'll take the stew," Matt replied, wishing she would just go away. No matter what he said, she would have an equal, if not stronger, response. Why was it their verbal sparring left him feeling edgy?

"Coming right up," she said, a fake brightness in her voice as she turned and walked away.

His eyes were tantalized by the swing of her hips and the rounded curve of her rear, leaving him even more frustrated. He wanted her to go away, yet he couldn't help but be attracted at the same time.

"So why do you think she's still here in town? You and I both heard her say she was on her way to Denver," he asked Jesse.

"Simple. Fran told me that her wallet was stolen on the bus."

For a moment that shocked him. He stopped and considered the situation. Is that why she fainted that night? Had she just discovered she had no cash, no identification, nothing?

"We have a bank. She could have withdrawn more cash. Did she report her wallet stolen?"

"I don't know. Why don't you ask her? Maybe she didn't have the money to leave," Jesse said gazing at his friend. "Maybe all the money she had in this world was in her wallet? Why are you being so hard on this girl? I wouldn't move in with McKenzie if I were going to be investigated and interrogated by her lawyer brother."

"McKenzie is not thinking straight, and someone has to look out for her."

But it was more than that. He felt drawn to the beautiful Valerie Brown, and yet he felt repelled at the same time. He didn't' know enough about her. And he didn't like her staying with his sister.

"I understand, but there is only so much you can do for McKenzie. She has to make her own decisions."

"Maybe, but as her attorney, I recommend a criminal background check and a credit check. Plus I would have asked for references."

Jesse started to laugh. "Matt, your clients are getting to you. You're being a little too suspicious."

"Maybe I just want to make sure my sister isn't harboring a fugitive," Matt replied, knowing he somehow had to convince Jesse to do a search on Valerie Brown.

"So what's going to satisfy you that she's just a woman in need of a job?" Jesse asked.

Ah, the perfect opening.

"Verification that she is who she says she is. Check out Valerie Brown, and let me know what you find," Matt said. "If her wallet was stolen, I'm sure she would have let DPS know that her license is missing since she didn't let you know."

"Sure," Jesse said. His lips curved up in a smile. "It will also show any outstanding warrants."

Matt shrugged. "At least I'll know that she's not Lizzie Borden's great-granddaughter."

Jesse shook his head. "Okay, on one condition."

"What's that?" Matt asked.

"That you will accept Valerie for who she says she is and drop this."

Matt frowned. "As long as I know you have the right Valerie Brown."

"Man, you are impossible. Don't be surprised if you

find out that Valerie Brown has no record and really does live in Phoenix, Arizona."

Right, Matt thought. "Yeah, and don't be shocked if my instincts are right. She's hiding something. I don't know what. She had no intention of staying here, and yet she's serving chow at Fran's diner."

"That's what happens when you have no money," Jesse replied. He glanced over to where Valerie was serving the loggers. "And the men in the area are going to get fat from coming to Fran's every day."

Why did it frustrate Matt whenever he saw other men appreciate Valerie's looks? She was probably a high school dropout, running some kind of con. He would do well to remember that behind that polished smile was no Mensa member.

Chapter Five

Three days later, the brisk January wind slashed right through Matt as he scurried into the warm café. An eerie glow radiated from the frost-blanketed windows.

He opened the door, and the tinkling bell announced his arrival. He searched for the one woman he couldn't shake from his mind. Fran stood next to a table taking an order, but Valerie was nowhere in sight. He breathed a sigh of relief and saw Jesse at their table, nursing a cup of steaming coffee.

Matt hurried over to his friend, who had his face buried inside the *Denver Daily News*.

"Hey man," Matt called as he slid into the booth.

"You gotta read how this woman got revenge on her fiancé," Jesse said as he handed him the newspaper.

Matt shrugged out of his coat and glanced at the paper, wanting to get to the real reason he was here. "Give me the scoop."

"This woman in Dallas set fire to her fiancé's Corvette," Jesse said, his voice rising with indignation. "A classic 1965."

"Is she nuts?" Matt exclaimed.

Jesse shook his head. "She must be. The paper says the couple were to be married. Five minutes before the ceremony, she rushed out of the church and drove off in his Corvette. Later authorities found the car burning."

"I hope they arrested her!"

"No, the paper says she's a person of interest they want to talk to. Seems she's disappeared."

Valerie walked up. "Hello, Mr. Jordan, what can I get you?"

She was here. Her voice drew him, and he gazed into her cornflower eyes, which twinkled with warmth and laughter. "You can start by calling me Matt. And then I'd like some coffee."

"All rightee, Matt."

Why did the sound of her voice, deep and melodious, send delicious shivers down his spine?

She stepped over to a serving area and grabbed a pot of coffee. She returned, flipped his cup up, and began to pour the hot liquid.

Jesse shook his head. "That's cold blooded. Torching your fiancé's '65 Corvette."

Matt watched as she stared at Jesse in horror, her mouth open in shock, while the coffee overflowed from Matt's cup. Coffee splashed onto the table and ran unchecked onto his lap. The hot liquid stung as it hit Matt's thigh area.

"Hey!"

Suddenly she realized what she'd done. "Oh my gosh, I'm so sorry."

Valerie grabbed a napkin, setting the pot down on the table, and started dabbing at Matt's thigh.

He took a deep breath and tried not to react to the touch of her hands on his leg. The close proximity of the table and the booth had her near enough he could smell her bold, flowery perfume.

But worse, he had an excellent view down the front of her sweater and the lacy pink bra that covered her luscious breasts. Those breasts swayed with the motion of her body, and her hands were close enough to a certain area of his anatomy that he had to bite back a groan.

The napkin brushed the zipper of his jeans, and he could feel himself hardening. He grabbed her hand and took a shaky breath. "I'm fine."

"I'm so sorry, Matt. Are you sure I didn't burn you?"

Two inches higher and there could have been some serious damage, but his jeans had protected his skin from the hot coffee, just not from the appeal of Valerie.

"I'm okay. My jeans soaked up most of the liquid." She

stared at him worriedly.

He gritted out. "I'm all right."

She wiped up the coffee she had spilled on the table and then gave him an awkward look. "If you need anything else, just wave."

Jesse was trying hard not to laugh. "Are you okay?"

Matt growled. "Two inches higher and I would be singing soprano."

Jesse smiled and shook his head. "I'm sorry, but I couldn't tell if you were in physical pain or having your own personal meltdown."

"I think it was a little of both. She was practically in my lap, with her hands rubbing a little too close for comfort."

"Maybe I should get you two a room at the Springtown Inn so you can finish what she started."

"Like that's going to happen." Though it was a pleasant thought. Matt took a deep, relaxing breath and pushed the still-dry newspaper aside. "Let's get to the real reason why I'm here. What did you find out?"

Jesse took a sip of his coffee and his eyes darkened. "That you are a suspicious lawyer who needs to quit being so stubborn. Valerie Brown has no record."

"Yeah, but I mean did you find her in the system?"

"I found hundreds of Valerie Browns. None of them were serial killers or axe murderers. One had been married five times, but since she was in her fifties, I don't think it's the same Valerie."

Matt leaned back and frowned. His glance slid over to the girl across the room. She smiled and chatted while she filled the other guests' coffee cups. She seemed like a natural in the café. "Maybe I've been a little over the top regarding her. If she hadn't moved in with McKenzie, it wouldn't have mattered whether she stayed in town."

"I've been thinking about that." Jesse paused and took a sip of coffee. "Have you ever considered that having another woman there might be good for McKenzie? They can do that female bonding thing that women like to do."

"Maybe."

"You don't sound very convinced."

"If it was a woman I knew, I wouldn't care. But I don't know anything about Valerie." He sipped from his coffee and sighed. "McKenzie has made it very clear that it's her decision. Fran certainly seems to like the girl. I'm the only person in town who hasn't fallen under her spell, and even I could be susceptible, if I'd let myself."

"From watching the two of you just a minute ago, I'd say things were a little hot."

Matt frowned at his friend's joke. "The only thing hot was the coffee."

Jesse grinned. "Give it a week or two, and who knows? Valerie may decide small-town life is boring and move on."

Matt thought for a moment and once again wondered why he was having such a reaction to this woman. Something in his gut warned him that she wasn't who she said she was.

"Over the years, I have learned to hone in on my instincts when alarm bells are going off. And they clang in my head whenever she's around."

"You should see a doctor about that," the sheriff teased.

"Funny."

"Maybe those warning bells are because you're attracted to our cute little waitress."

Matt opened his mouth to protest, took one look at Jesse's smiling face, and knew he'd be wasting his time. And no matter how much he wanted to deny it, he *was* attracted to Valerie. Instead he scowled at his friend, giving him his best lawyer warning face that he used at trial.

Jesse looked sheepish. "Of course, I'm sure it has something to do with you wanting to protect McKenzie."

"Of course it does," Matt said. He was tired of fighting a battle over Valerie he wasn't winning with McKenzie, Jesse, or anyone at the café, and he hated to admit that maybe they were right. "In the meantime, I'll stop in to see McKenzie and the kids more often. Which is going to take me away from the office more, and right now I don't have the time."

"What happened to you hiring some part-time help?"

Valerie strolled up, making Matt instantly aware of her presence. "More coffee, gentlemen?"

Jesse grinned at her. "Sure. But in my cup, please."

"Cute. It was my first spill as a waitress," she said, pouring his coffee. "How about you, Matt?"

"I'm wearing all the caffeine I need."

"This time I'll put it in your cup."

"That would be nice."

She glanced at the newspaper lying on the table. "Are you through with that newspaper, Jesse? Fran wanted me to save it."

"Sure." He handed her the newspaper.

Matt watched Valerie walk away, enjoying the sway of her jeans before he turned his attention back to Jesse. "Do you know any teenagers that might be looking for a part-time clerical job? Someone who could do data entry and filing? I need someone who can file, do spreadsheets and general office work for twenty hours a week."

Valerie stopped in her tracks and faced him. "I can do those things."

His eyes met and held hers. "I don't think so."

She shrugged. "Suit yourself. I graduated summa cum laude from college last year. I was going to start…"

She halted, her forehead creasing in thought as she quickly clammed up.

His Mensa comment haunted him, and he realized he had so misjudged her. Not only did she not have a criminal background, she was a college graduate. Usually he could read people very well, so why had he missed with Valerie?

Still, the lawyer in him knew that she wasn't telling everything, but then, who did?

"Gotta run, guys. Table three is calling me."

He watched her go, more intrigued with her every day.

"Why didn't you offer her the job?" Jesse asked, his voice incredulous.

"It wouldn't work."

"What do you mean it wouldn't work? You have a college graduate that obviously needs the money. She's the one you need to hire."

"If I can't trust her with my sister, why in the hell do you think I'm going to trust her with my business?"

"Because you're working on your paranoia, and you need the help. And so far you have nothing to show for your suspicions except that it illustrates how much your job is getting to you."

"Thanks for the vote of confidence." He frowned, realizing that what Jesse said must be true for him to act so distrusting of Valerie. She was a beautiful girl down on her luck, and he wanted to make her out to be a criminal.

"Well, listen to yourself. You have the perfect candidate, and you're afraid to hire her. Lighten up, man. The girl needs a break."

Matt thought of his upcoming caseload and the mounting work. "I do have the Gilmore case coming up next month, and I still have a lot of research to do."

"Then hire some kid from the local high school who you're going to pay to play around on the Internet. They won't get half the work done that a more mature college graduate could accomplish."

"Go screw yourself, Jesse."

"I'd have a better chance than getting through your thick skull." He paused. "Besides, most of the kids are more into the ski season than working."

The last time he'd used a teenager to do his filing, he'd found the kid didn't really know the alphabet. Not to mention the fact he'd caught him with his girlfriend at the office. Matt frowned. He didn't have time for a lot of nonsense.

He motioned Valerie to their table.

"Yes, gentlemen?"

Matt noticed how she seemed not to have a care in the world. "How fast can you type?"

"I haven't been timed in a long time, but probably around 75 words a minute."

Jesse let out a whistle.

"Have you ever typed legal briefs before?"

She paused. "No."

"The position is only twenty hours a week."

"Why are you telling me? You don't want to hire me."

"Maybe I reacted a little too quickly."

"Maybe I've changed my mind," she retorted.

"Maybe you have. But it pays fifteen dollars an hour."

Valerie stopped and contemplated that information.

She put her hands on her hips. "We don't like each other. What makes you think we could work together?"

He frowned at her question. She believed in going for the jugular. "Who said I didn't like you?"

She counted off on her fingers. "One, trying to convince your sister to kick me out. Two, thinking I would steal from McKenzie. Three, talking about me to Jesse and Fran. And four, wondering why I was still here. Want to try for five?"

Jesse cleared his throat. "She's got a point, man."

Matt shrugged. "So I'm overprotective of my sister. That doesn't mean that we can't work together. My house is big enough that you could work in the kitchen and I'll take the office. We won't even share a room."

"You're not afraid I'm going to put all your Post-it Notes on the black market?"

He laughed and gazed into her blue eyes. He really wasn't concerned about her stealing. He still thought she was hiding something, but maybe keeping a close tab on her would be best. He could get to know more about her and find out just why she'd decided to stay.

"I didn't know there was a black market for Post-it Notes. Maybe you can hook me up," he said, responding to her challenge.

"Glue shortage." She bit her bottom lip, her brows drawn together in concentration. "I could still work here at the café?"

"Sure. I can work around Fran's schedule." He could see the money had tweaked her interest. "We could try it for just a few days to see how it works out."

"On one condition."

"What's that?"

"You pay me in cash, no questions asked."

"That's illegal," he said, knowing he was allowed so much contract labor, but hoping that she would give him her legal information.

"You're the lawyer. You figure out a way to make it work."

He smiled at her response. "Can you start tomorrow?"

"I'll be there right after the lunch rush."

After she walked off, Matt turned to Jesse. "I hope I have not made a colossal mistake that I'm going to regret."

~

As soon as she could, Valerie took the newspaper and went into the restroom. She shut and locked the door of the stall. She flipped through the paper until she found the small paragraph. She read through the article and breathed a sigh of relief. They listed her first name, not her middle name. They were searching for Diane Burrows. For once going by her middle name had paid off. In the past she'd hated that they called her by her middle name. But not this time.

The article was more humorous than newsworthy and said only that the bride-to-be, Diane Burrows, was a person of interest.

When Jesse mentioned the article, she'd almost fainted, and after spilling coffee in Matt's lap…well, she now had no doubt the man filled his jeans out very nicely.

God, what was she thinking? A week away from her disastrous wedding and already she was dwelling on the pants worn by yet another lawyer. No more lawyers.

Yet oddly enough, she didn't miss Carter. They were supposed to be on their honeymoon, and somehow she didn't miss Carter or the Caribbean. Instead she felt a sense of relief at being here, though working in the café was harder than she'd ever labored before, and now she would be taking a second job.

Her father would be shocked to learn she was doing menial labor.

Working with Matt would build her cash much quicker and get her to Denver, where she could once again start her journey to a different nowhere.

But working beside the handsome lawyer was going to be a challenge. Especially when he said he trusted her. Ha! He'd had his lawyer face on, and she knew she had her battle cut out for her to convince him that she was just plain Valerie Brown, needing to make an extra buck.

She'd soon have him eating out of her hand, believing her, and when she had enough cash, she'd be out of here. And though it would be hard to leave Fran and McKenzie, putting as much distance as she could between her and Matt would be a good thing.

The sexual attraction she felt for him was just that,

sexual. She didn't need to be involved with anymore freakin' lawyers, or even men for that matter. It was time to get her head on straight without a man to muddy up the process.

Now all she had to do was hang on until she had enough money to leave.

~

Valerie rang the bell of Matt's little house right off Main Street. It wasn't anything fancy, just a quaint frame home that appeared comfortable. The sort of place people used for offices. A sign in the front yard read Matt Jordan, Attorney at Law. She'd cringed when she saw that sign, another law office, but quickly remembered he would be paying her double what she earned at the café.

Being without her trust fund was an awakening life experience. What little she made didn't go far enough, and she knew until the wedding fiasco, she'd lived a very indulgent lifestyle. Color her spoilt. But she was learning to make do.

She rang the bell again, and finally he opened the door, a portable phone to his ear. He motioned her in while he explained the legal process to a client.

"I have requisitioned the paperwork from his attorney, and we should have that any day now."

The front room had a desk with a flat-screen computer monitor swimming amongst the scattered papers and files. Valerie thought of her father's desk in his office on the twenty-second floor of the Trammel Crow Center in downtown Dallas. The gleaming mahogany of his desk never looked like this.

At the thought of her father, sadness swept through her, and she quickly pushed the thought away. Regardless of what had happened, she missed him.

A stack of papers with a big accordion file folder on top

had a sticky note that said, "file." She picked up the papers and began to put them in the appropriate slots by the clients' last names. The stack included everything from divorces to wills, and even a few civil suits.

By the time Matt hung up the phone and turned around to speak to her, she had the stack all sorted and ready to file away.

"What are you doing?" he asked.

"I'm sorting your filing."

"How do you know how I like it filed?"

"Well, most offices file by the client's last name. Is your method different?" she asked.

He frowned at her. "No. I'm surprised you knew what to do."

"Filing doesn't take a degree in astrophysics."

He gazed at her, and she warmed under his perusal, his green eyes dancing with laughter.

"Where are the files kept?" she asked, needing him to stop staring at her like she was a ripe peach ready for the plucking.

"Let me show you around," he said.

He took her through the house. "The front room is where I receive clients. The back of the house is where I live. I turned one of the bedrooms into my file room."

She followed him down a hall into the kitchen, which had a small den on the back of the room. A rock fireplace sat in the middle of the wall, with bookshelves on either side. A plasma television occupied a central spot with a pit group in the middle of the room. There was a warm, cozy feeling about the room, and she liked his taste in furniture.

Another hall off the kitchen led to the back of the house. "The file room is down the hall here and across from it is the guest room, and then my bedroom is at the end."

"I won't go past the file room," she said.

"You will if you want to go to the restroom," he responded.

"You've got a point."

They entered the filing room, where cabinets lined the walls. Folders were stacked two feet high on each cabinet, waiting to be replaced.

She glanced at him in disapproval. "So who has done your filing?"

"Well…let's just say that I'm not always very good at putting files back."

"That's an understatement."

"When I decided to move from Denver, I never expected to do much work here in this little town, but I've been surprised at the business I've received."

"Do you travel to Denver much?"

"Oh yeah. Whenever I have a trial going on. I've got one coming up in the next two months, so I'll be traveling back and forth."

Great. When it came time to leave town, she could disappear while he was gone. Maybe she'd go to Canada or maybe New York. Anywhere but Dallas, Texas.

"I need you to sign a confidentiality agreement," he told her.

She couldn't contain the *duh* expression from appearing on her face. How dumb did he think she was? No, he didn't know that she'd grown up around lawyers, but anyone with a pea-size brain would know to keep their mouth shut about what they saw or heard in an attorney's office.

"The only thing I talk about in the café is the weather and the specials of the day."

"Good. Keep it that way, but I still need the signed document."

She shrugged. "Not a problem." She glanced around the office, willing herself to begin the decluttering process. A mountain of filing awaited her, and she still had to prove to him that she wasn't a total idiot. "Where do you want me to begin?"

"See what you can do on the filing today, and we'll go from there."

The phone rang, and he glanced down at the caller ID on the receiver he held in his hand. "I need to get this. Are you going to be okay?"

"I'll be fine." She shooed him out the door, ready for him to take his sweet-smelling self out of her sight. Why did she notice the tempting aroma that came from his big frame? It was an alluring smell, and she didn't need the distraction.

He answered the phone. She fished out her ear buds from her iPod Nano and wedged them into her ears. She needed a diversion from the handsome lawyer. She hit the Play button.

~

An hour later, Matt peeked in the door and felt like a giant fist slammed into his chest. He couldn't breathe. Valerie was bent over, her sexy little derriere in the air as she twisted and danced while she put folders into the file drawers. The jeans she wore curved around her buttocks and danced enticingly before him.

She rose, shook her hair, and sang to the music. Her voice was on key as she sang, unaware of him watching her. She picked up another stack of file folders and began to shake her hips while she put them in the cabinet.

He'd never seen anyone dance and sing while filing. And it gave a whole new meaning to working. He stepped into the room, intent upon touching her to let her know he was there. She whirled around and slammed right into him, her soft breasts snug against his chest.

He wanted to groan, while she gasped in fright.

"Geez, Louise, you could let a girl know you were

there."

"I was trying to, but you were obviously into your work."

She hit the Stop button on her iPod and pulled the ear buds from her ears.

"I don't do dull, and filing is dull, so I found a way to make it more fun."

He smiled, wanting to join in her fun. "I see that. I'm getting worried that maybe I should take out workers' comp insurance, in case you throw your backside out."

She grinned. "My backside is perfectly fine."

Oh God, she could say that again. He might need to take out insurance on himself if he had to watch her dancing much more. How was he going to take seeing her each day? And now she stood less than a foot away from him. He could smell her hair. Without thinking, he reached out and brushed a strand that was on her cheek away from her face. Her skin was soft and her blue eyes dilated.

The gesture seemed intimate, and he swallowed to regain his composure.

He took a step back, needing space. "I came by to check on you, but you seem to be doing just fine without me, so I'll let you get back to it."

She didn't say anything, but put the ear plugs back in her ears, hit the play button and picked up another stack of files.

Maybe this wasn't such a good idea after all. Maybe he should hire someone else. Maybe he should just take her right here on the floor and get it out of his system.

He groaned quietly and returned to his desk. Twenty hours a week with Valerie. Twenty hours a week of her long legs and cute rear end swaying around his office. Twenty hours of the sweet smells of lilacs and roses drifting through the office just might be the death of him.

Chapter Six

Three weeks passed with Valerie working in the office four days a week. Matt anticipated her every afternoon, when she would walk over from the café immediately after the lunch rush. Matt kept her busy until time for the supper crowd. Of course, a rush in this small town was anything more than ten customers at a time. And lately, much to Matt's disgust, the café seemed to draw every male within fifty miles or farther.

In the time they'd spent together, he had learned very little about her other than she liked to listen to pop music and she tried to make everything fun. She could turn the most mundane task into something that kept her entertained. He'd watched her do the *hip-hop file dance, the type-a-page-and-twirl-in-her-chair routine, the research smash, and boogie-woogie cleanup.*

All of which left him a might edgy and more than a little aroused. Nothing could be more exciting than to watch a woman dance when she didn't think anyone was watching her. And Valerie did a lot of dancing, moving, swaying, and shaking, which left him using more than his normal amount of cold water in winter.

They spoke only about business, and he had determined that the iPod constantly in her ear was a defensive wall to keep boundaries between them. She couldn't hear him, and therefore they didn't talk. Soon, very soon, he was going to burst through that wall to the other side.

After the first week, he'd realized Valerie knew what she was doing and wondered if she had some sort of law background. She didn't bother him with the normal newbie questions. When she had to admit to needing a response from him, her questions were technical and precise. More knowledgeable than the average person who'd never been around the law.

Matt knew he had misjudged this woman badly, and that surprised him. In the past he'd always read people very well, but Valerie had somehow slid beneath his radar. She was definitely not what he expected. And the changes she created in his office were those of an individual who knew how a law practice operated. Now there was organized chaos instead of a disorganized mess. Files were in their proper location, and she'd even created a checkout system. That way she knew whenever he had a file, just like in his office in downtown Denver.

Every day he feared he was becoming a little more dependent on her, and the walls of doubt he'd erected about her were crumbling.

He strode over to her desk and tapped her on the shoulder.

"How's it going?" he asked when she looked up from the monitor.

"Great. I should be finished in ten minutes."

"Good. Are you going back to the café tonight?"

"Yes, I've got to help Fran."

He gazed at her as she sat behind the desk he'd bought for her, wanting to know more about her, wanting her to open up to him, tell him who she was.

She returned to typing, and he couldn't restrain himself any longer. He sat on top of her desk in her direct line of her sight, where she was unable to avoid him.

Her brows raised in a quizzical expression, partly annoyance, partly curiosity.

"Is there something else you need?"

He tilted his head and studied her, wondering how he could get her to open up to him. What were the right things to say to Valerie Brown that would unlock her hidden secrets?

"That first night you were in town, was your wallet stolen on that bus?"

She bit her lip and glanced at her keyboard before she looked back up at him.

"Yes."

"So that's why you stayed in town."

"Yes."

He shook his head. "I guess that answers my question about why you're here. Why didn't you tell me?"

She smiled. "It was none of your business."

He chuckled, his insides tightening as he realized she was a tougher witness than anyone he'd ever cross-examined on a witness stand.

"Okay," he said, wondering how she'd respond to his next question. "Who did you work for before you came to Springtown?"

She smiled and slowly pulled her iPod earbuds from her ear. "If I told you, I'd have to kill you."

For a moment he was silent, hoping she would offer the information, but she wasn't giving anything away.

Staring into the sapphire depths of her eyes, he wanted to get lost in them, but wanted to know more about this woman. "Somewhere there's a lawyer who is missing his office help. Really, I can tell you have law office experience."

Her fingers paused on the keyboard, and she studied him for a moment. "I put myself through college as a lawyer's secretary."

"How long did you work for him?" he asked, thinking finally they were getting somewhere. "What was his name?"

"He was from the law office of TMI."

It took him about thirty seconds to realize she wasn't going to answer. "I've never heard of the law firm of Too Much Information. Are they large or small?"

She ignored him.

"What's the big deal about telling me where you

worked?"

"Nothing, except that it drives you crazy and gives me an air of mystery," she said, her voice teasing. "And I prefer to remain secretive."

Grinning, he admitted, "You're right, it does. I guess your mom and dad were pleased that you graduated college."

She turned and gave him a long stare, her brows furrowing as if she couldn't believe his audacity. "Do I need to bring the lamp over and let you shine it in my face, or are you going to start pulling my fingernails out if I don't answer your questions?"

He crossed his arms over his chest, leaned back, and surveyed her with his best drop-your-defenses smile. She was such a sassy little thing, and that challenged him. "I just wanted to know more about you. You drop in here on a bus, yet you obviously have skills and are an educated, bright young woman."

"Maybe I'm an environmentalist? Riding a bus, saving the planet with fewer emissions. Or maybe I'm just into making money. If I'm so bright, when do I get a raise?"

He laughed, knowing she had a quick mind with a comeback for everything. She parried very well with words, and it kind of excited him. Verbal sparring with her left him feeling upbeat, stimulated, and ready for the next challenge. But what did it do for her?

She gazed at him, her blue eyes twinkling. "Does this mean you no longer think I'm going to rob your sister blind?"

"I was only trying to protect McKenzie." He seriously wanted her to realize he'd protect McKenzie and the children at any cost.

After working with her every day, he didn't worry about her trustworthiness anymore, but he remained curious as to her background. She seemed such a mystery, and he was intrigued enough to want to know more.

"Oh, so now it's safe to steal the silver."

He shook his head at her. "Ha ha! I don't think McKenzie has any silver."

"Too bad" A fake disappointed frown settled on her face. "There's no room in my suitcase for nasty silver I don't want or need."

The thought of her leaving suddenly sent his spirits plummeting. He didn't want her to leave, and the realization shocked him. Somehow during the last three weeks, he'd fallen under the same spell as everyone else. She had managed to get under his skin, and though he'd tried to resist, he liked her.

"Are you planning on going somewhere?" he asked, trying not to appear anxious. He'd just gotten his office somewhat organized, his work at least tolerable, and he didn't want to lose her help. Not to mention how much he enjoyed spending time with her.

Who was he kidding? He didn't want her to go.

"Not now. Someday, but not now," she said matter-of-factly. "But I am taking the day off on Monday."

He frowned, afraid suddenly of her leaving town and never seeing her again. "Why?"

"I've worked nonstop for a month, and I think it's time to go play." She smiled. "The ski resort is having a play day for the town. Half-price tickets for residents of Springtown."

"Oh," he said. He hadn't gone skiing at all this season. There was too much work and not enough time. "Where did you learn how to ski?"

She started to respond, and then her lips curved into a smile as she realized his tactic. "You must be a very good lawyer."

"Why do you say that?"

"Because you have a way of prying without the person

realizing what you're doing."

"Maybe," he admitted. "But I'd like to know more about you."

"Why should I tell you more? You have never told me anything about you."

"What do you want to know? I was born in Denver. When I was eight, McKenzie was born, and my dad left us a year later. My mother struggled to support us. When I was eighteen, I went to the University of Colorado on scholarship. Soon after, I attended Southern Methodist University law school in Dallas, and when I graduated from there, I came back to Denver and went to work for the largest liability law office in the state."

"That's a brief synopsis counselor, but you didn't tell me how the divorce of your parents affected you. You must have been an overprotective brother even then since you are today. No wives, no girlfriends? You didn't tell me about you, Matt."

He took a deep breath and tried to switch the subject. "So what about you?"

His breath caught the smell of spring, and his pulse quickened as she shook her long blonde hair away from her face. "Okay. I was born to Jeff and Mabel Brown in Phoenix, Arizona. My parents died in a car accident when I was eighteen. I attended the University of Arizona in Tucson and graduated last year. And here I am."

"You didn't really tell me any personal information either."

She smiled knowingly, her eyes twinkling with laughter. "No, I didn't."

He wanted to press her further, but knew that in doing so, he would only make her more resistant. And what would he do with the information anyway? He'd promised Jesse to drop the matter, and he had every intention of doing so. Yet that tiny voice inside him wanted him to continue to learn about this girl. There was something about her that didn't fit the profile she gave, and he was curious as to why.

They sat awkwardly, each waiting for the other to say something but neither one budging.

Wanting to test her, he said, "I heard the Jayhawks have a really good football team this year."

She shook her head at him. "And I hear SMU is rebuilding its team."

Anyone who followed football knew that the Arizona team wasn't the Jayhawks. The University of Kansas was the Jayhawks. Did she just let the slip go, or had she really not graduated from Arizona?

He watched her trying to determine if she'd lied about the university. "Actually I follow Colorado more than I do SMU."

"Did you like living in Dallas?" she asked.

"It was all right. A little too hot for my comfort, but the city itself was nice."

"How about Tucson? Did you like living there?" he asked her, needing more information from her.

"Oh yeah, the city was beautiful, and the mountains were great, though not as many pine trees as here."

Mountains? Pine trees? Sure you could see the mountains, but Tucson was only twenty miles from Phoenix. And the air was just as hot and dry there as in Phoenix. It was desert surrounded by dry hills and no sign of pine trees. Cactus, but not pine trees.

He didn't say anything. Maybe she considered those hills mountains. Maybe she considered cactus as pine trees, or maybe she'd lied. But the city wasn't nestled among the mountains like here in Springtown. Or maybe Valerie Brown had never lived in Tucson.

Another incongruity.

"So you're skiing on Monday."

                    Sylvia McDaniel

"Yep. I can't wait."

"I'll let you get back to work."

Matt walked out of her office. She was lying about Tucson. He'd watched his father lie for years. He'd seen how the pain of his father's lies had affected his mother. He didn't like liars.

~

Valerie skied off the lift smoothly, her rented skis not nearly as nice as her own Volki Supersport series at home, but she had to make do with what she could get.

McKenzie had lent her a jacket and ski pants, and she'd rented the boots and skis. She skied away from the lift chair, testing the skis and stretching her legs. She stopped at the large map at the top of the mountain and considered her choices of trails. It had been a year since she'd skied, so she chose a green route, for beginners, to warm up her legs. She pushed off and slid away. The swish of her skis in her ears, the clean smell of the pine trees, and nothing but blue sky above her. The land around her was beautiful, all pristine white, yet the sun felt warm on her face, and the day couldn't have been more beautiful.

For the first time since the wedding, she felt alive, more like the old Valerie.

Easily she moved through the crowded green trail, turning the tips of her skis as she wound her way down the mountain.

When she arrived at the bottom, she hopped on the lift back up the mountain. It was always more fun to ski with family and friends, and she missed her father skiing by her side. He'd taught her to ski at Vail, Colorado, and had taken her to Switzerland when she'd proven she could ski any trail with confidence.

The thought of how her father had taken Carter's side still left a hole in her heart. She missed him. Several times she'd been tempted to pick up the phone and call him but stopped, knowing it was too soon and they both needed more time. Over a month had passed since the near wedding, and she wasn't ready to forgive and forget. Sooner or later she would have to deal with what she'd done to Carter's Corvette, but right now she preferred later.

Her actions had been impulsive, and she'd been wrong, but she wasn't ready to face either her father or Carter. The jerk deserved that and more. He was lucky she hadn't neutered him with the cake knife.

Yet more than anything, her pain was from her father's betrayal and not Carter's, and that amazed her. If she'd loved Carter, wouldn't his infidelity hurt the most? Yet she rarely thought of Carter.

With a swish she skied off the lift, determined to take the blue intermediate trail. She turned toward the more challenging trail with her skis pointed downward. Out of nowhere a guy shot toward her, coming dangerously close. Before she could swerve out of the way, he clipped her right ski, sending her tumbling. Their skis tangled together, and the two of them went sliding down the mountain.

When they stopped, she felt a rush of anger. "You Jerk! You could have killed us! Have you heard of yelling 'on your right'?"

The man's face was buried in her jacket. He raised his head and before he pushed back his goggles, she knew who was behind those dark lenses.

Matt removed his goggles and grinned at her, sending her blood pressure climbing. The oaf had followed her.

"Actually, I was trying to catch up to you. I hit a bump in the snow and lost it."

"From the looks of it, you never had control."

"Hey, I'm a pretty good skier."

"Don't try out for the Olympics."

They were lying in the snow half on one another. She

could feel his chest, and though there were layers of clothes between them, their bodies were so close it felt intimate. Her breath quickened and a tingle wove its way down her spine.

She didn't need this. She moved, trying to untangle their skis and separate their bodies, anxious to put space between them. Her ski lost its grip and she felt her body start to slide. She planted her downhill ski and then raised herself up.

"Are you okay? I didn't hurt you, did I?" he asked.

"I'm fine. What about you?"

"I left my pride back up the mountain, but other than that, I'll live."

She planted her pole in the snow to keep her steady. "That's not all you left up the hill, but we won't go there. What are you doing here?"

"You mentioned skiing, and well, I sat in that office all by myself and I thought 'hey, I'm going skiing too.' So here I am."

He stood and brushed the snow off his suit.

She shook her head. "Do you have health insurance?"

"Of course," he replied.

"Good. You might need it."

"I'll see you down at the bottom, and then we'll find a black trail." He took off like a flash, and she couldn't resist the challenge.

She soon sped past him and stood waiting for him down by the lift.

He skied up to her, huffing and out of breath. Without a word they got in line for the lift and skied up to the chair. When they were whisked away, he turned to her.

"So where did you learn to ski that way?"

She gave him a teasing smile. "Oh, around. I'm not answering any questions today, counselor."

He shook his head. "You are so not who you appear to

be."

"What do you mean by that?"

"Well, first you surprised me by knowing the law. And now you ski like a gold medalist. You continue to astonish me."

"My father trained me." Of course, she didn't want to mention that her father tried out for the Olympic ski team in college and would have made it except for an injury that sidelined him.

"And who was your daddy?"

"I told you already," she remembered the lie.

"Yeah, you did."

The lift approached the drop-off location, and they both skied smoothly away from the chair.

The ski resort photographer stepped in front of them. "Get close together."

Valerie opened her mouth to protest, but before she could say no, Matt leaned in close for the photo.

The woman snapped the picture. What could a photo hurt? After all she would only be here another month at the longest, and he knew what she looked like.

"You can pick up a copy any time after two," the photographer said.

Like that was going to happen, Valerie thought.

After the photographer moved on, she glanced at Matt. "Are you up for a black run?"

"As long as there are no moguls. I don't do moguls."

"Me neither. I like to ski downhill fast."

"Let's go down Screaming Eagle."

"Meet you at the bottom." She pointed her skis down the mountain, skiing parallel, making smooth curves straight down the steep incline. Halfway to the bottom she stopped and waited for him to catch up.

He skidded to a halt beside her. They were the only people on the trail, and the wind whispered through the pines, soothing her.

"Wow, I'd forgotten how much fun this can be. I get so involved with my cases that sometimes I forget about the pleasures in life."

"My new motto is If it's not fun, I'm not doing it," she said as she stared into his eyes. His cheeks were flushed from the cold, his green eyes twinkled, and he appeared relaxed and so sexually stimulating that Valerie had to take a deep breath.

"You need to do this more often." She reached out and brushed snow from his hair before she realized what she'd done. Quickly, she jerked her hand back. "You look like you're having fun instead of all stressed and lawyerly."

"I'm having a great time," he said, then glanced at her sheepishly. "I hope you don't mind that I sort of intruded on your day."

"Hey, if I get tired of you, I know how to ski away."

"I hope you don't."

She stared at him, an awareness of him as a man leaving her a little breathless. This was just for today. They would have a good time and tomorrow, return to normal. "I'm going down."

"Oh, yeah," he said. "Eat my snow."

He took off and she gave him a head start. Then she sped after him, catching him toward the bottom of the trail. When she reached his side, she stopped and intentionally slid her ski over his, toppling him over, taking him down.

Once again they were a tumble of skis, arms, and legs. Valerie giggled as she landed on top of him.

"I owed you that one." She laughed.

Their eyes connected and the laughing stopped. Her mouth was a mere inch from his lips, and she watched his tongue moisten their fullness. Heat, a hot, molten fire of desire raced through her, chasing the chill away.

She couldn't live another thirty seconds without

knowing his kiss. Without knowing if this was real or just a rebound kiss. She had to know now.

Grasping his head, she pulled him to her, her lips covering his, needing an answer. His mouth was warm and moist, and she couldn't help but wonder if the heat generated from the two of them would melt the snow and start a flash flood.

At first his kiss was soft and tentative, but then he grew more certain, deepening the kiss, his lips demanding, seeking, pressuring her. She opened her mouth wider for him, and his tongue caressed hers, eliciting a moan from deep inside her. God, he tasted good. He smelled good. She grabbed his jacket and pulled him into her, but their suits got in the way. She needed him closer. She needed to touch him. She needed him, now.

The swish of other skiers passing them entered her fogged brain, and she heard a man yell, "Hey, get a room."

They broke apart. Stunned, she touched her hand to her lips. What was she doing? Had she lost her mind?

She was running from a relationship, not trying to find someone to connect with. And she'd kissed him.

Panic seized her by the throat, and she rose from the ground, focused on getting away from the emotions he evoked.

"Valerie?" he asked as she popped her ski back on.

She ignored him. With her boot firmly in her ski, she steadied her poles and pushed off. She skied as fast as safely possible down the rest of the mountain.

The kiss had been mind-blowing. It had been earth moving, shattering, and all those things that were not supposed to happen to her. Not with another lawyer. And Lord, it was much too soon to be thinking about yet another man in her life.

At the bottom of the mountain, she skied up to the chalet and halted. She yanked off her skis, turned them into the rental place, and jumped on the next bus returning to town.

He was a stinking lawyer who kissed like heaven, and she feared could distract her from her goal. She had to remain focused on earning enough money to leave this small Colorado town behind, along with sexy Matt Jordan.

No more men! No more lawyers!

Chapter Seven

When Valerie arrived at the law office the next day, Matt wasn't there. The door was unlocked, and a card lay on her desk. She tore open the envelope and pulled out the photo and a note.

Thanks for the great time skiing with you yesterday. Here is your copy of the photo. Let's go skiing again, soon. I had to go to Denver but hope to return day after tomorrow. Lock up when you leave.

The before-kiss picture caught them smiling, laughing, with flushed cheeks and noses rosy from the cold. They made a nice-looking couple. But that was the problem. They weren't a couple and would never be a couple. Barely a month had passed since her wedding fiasco. She refused to get involved with another lawyer.

She took a deep breath, taking in the scent of Matt permeating the office. A pleasant woodsy smell that lingered in his absence.

She had enjoyed the afternoon with Matt. Working with him, she had come to respect and admire his determination to defend his clients. Outside of work, he was fun, and from their time together, he gave the impression of a great guy. Too bad she hadn't met him before Carter.

And now by, leaving her alone in his office, he'd showed her she had gained his trust. He'd gone from a man determined to prove she was a criminal to entrusting her with his law practice. In the space of four weeks, he'd changed his mind about her, and while that should have made her feel good, she felt guilty.

Guilty for not telling him the truth. Guilty because he'd told her he did not condone liars. And she was living a lie.

With a sigh, she closed the card. What would he think when he learned that she'd not only lied about her identity and where she came from, but also that there could be a warrant out for her arrest?

What did it matter? She was here for only a short period of time, just until she decided to catch the next bus to Denver. Once she had sufficient cash to continue on her way, she would leave Matt and his law practice far behind.

With that resolution, she laid down the photo. Immediately she began to clear the latest files. Matt would return to the filing done, his calls answered, and the latest research requests completed.

She would do her job, but she refused to get involved with the man. No matter how much she enjoyed being with him, no matter how much fun they had together, they were not meant to be together. So why did the thought seem somehow depressing?

~

Two days later at closing time, Valerie swabbed the floor of the café. Outside the wind howled, rattling the windowpanes, and plunging the temperature below freezing. Blizzard warnings had cleared the streets. It wasn't a fit night for man or beast on the roads. And she worried about the whereabouts of Matt. He was due back today.

"Are you about finished?" Fran asked, coming from the kitchen with her coat on.

"Yeah. All I need to do is empty this bucket and grab my coat."

The front door burst open, and Matt blew in along with swirling snow. Valerie stopped and stared at him, relief surging through her. At the sight of him, an overwhelming urge to run and throw her arms around him almost overcame her, but she didn't.

It was the first time she'd seen him since their kiss. She'd tried to block his image from her mind and not think of the way his lips had felt against hers. But since the blizzard warning had been issued, she'd worried and hoped he'd stayed in Denver.

"Hi," he said. He sounded uncertain, standing in the door in his ski parka and boots.

Relief consumed her, and she stared at his anxious expression. How could she stay mad at him? All he'd done was return her kiss. And she hadn't exactly resisted the feel of his lips. In fact, she'd enjoyed those few moments of pleasure.

"Hi," she said, breathing like she'd run the mile. "You made it back."

"Just drove in. The roads are bad."

For several hours, snow had been falling, and when she looked out the window all she saw was a swirling mass of glittering snowflakes.

He shut the door but stayed in the entryway. "I don't want to get your clean floor dirty from my boots."

"What are you doing here on a night like tonight?" Fran asked, looking suspiciously between the two of them.

"I need to check on McKenzie and the kids. Make sure that the horses are taken care of and that they have everything they need. I thought I could save you the trip of driving Valerie to McKenzie's."

"Thank you, Jesus, you're a godsend. Even though it's not far, I was dreading having to drive in this mess." Fran strode over to Valerie and took the bucket she still held from her hands. "I'll finish up here. They say we're going to have three feet of snow by morning." She looked directly at Valerie. "Get going, and if it's bad, I won't be opening the café in the morning."

"Thanks, Fran," Valerie said. She gave Matt a quick glance. "Let me get my coat and gloves. I'm ready to go."

A tingle of excitement trickled through her as she slipped her coat on, pulled her gloves over her hands, and put a toboggan over her ears. Seeing him walk through that door had made her giddy with pleasure and relief. She tried to resist the feelings, but they refused to disappear.

Matt opened the door, and the two of them strode out into the blustery weather. The cold wind sliced through her as she hurried to Matt's Jeep. He opened the door, and she climbed into the vehicle, aware of the bone-chilling cold.

Matt scurried around and scrambled into the vehicle. She shivered as he started the Jeep and backed out, the tires sliding through the snow. He put the vehicle in four-wheel drive, and the Jeep pushed through the packed snow.

"It should be warm in a few minutes," he said.

Deserted streets glittered with the blanket of snow and gave the little town a winter postcard appearance. The windshield wipers barely kept the glass clear as the wind swirled the flakes in the headlights of the car.

"This is beautiful," she said, in awe of the power of nature.

"It's been years since we had a storm this big. They're warning about power outages." He motioned behind him, and she could see the back end loaded with firewood. "I wanted to make sure McKenzie had enough wood in case the power went out."

"When I left this morning she was headed to the store to make sure we had plenty of food. And she ordered more hay for the horses. She said she would put them in the barn at the first sign of snow."

"Good." He let out a long breath before he asked, "Did you find the card?"

"Yes, Matt, thank you." An awkward silence filled the Jeep. Her head overruled her heart. She'd made a vow to herself, and she intended to keep it. "You know, Matt, I think it would be best if we just remain friends."

"All good relationships start with friendship."

She smiled, her heart screaming at her to stop while her brain reminded her she was taking a sabbatical from men.

"We can't be more than friends."

"Why?" He glanced at her quickly. "You have a boyfriend somewhere?"

"There you go again with the questions."

"Is that unreasonable?" he asked.

"No."

"Well, do you?" He asked, demanding an answer. "I've thought about that kiss for the last two days. I couldn't wait to get home and see you."

Her heart did a little mambo dance. She'd thought of nothing else for the last two days.

"There's no boyfriend."

"So what's the problem? Even though you ran away, you responded like you enjoyed kissing me."

"Look, I like you. I think you're great, but nothing is going to happen between us," she said in the darkness of the Jeep, not responding to his comments about the kiss.

She genuinely liked Matt and felt attracted to him, but that didn't mean she wanted to act on this temptation. All she had to do was remind herself of his profession, and she knew there could never be anything between them.

Carter and her father were great reminders of the family of lawyers she'd come from, and she'd experienced the pain of their betrayal. Betrayal she never wanted to experience again.

Plus she'd lied to Matt. She was a fake and a liar, and she couldn't bring herself to tell him the truth. Not when their relationship had changed for the better. She didn't want him to hate her.

He turned down the lane to McKenzie's. "I think you're too late, Valerie. I think something has already happened between us."

She frowned and gave him her best back off look. "It's not a good idea, Matt."

"Yeah, well, bungee jumping isn't a great idea, but that

didn't stop me."

Shocked at the determination in his voice, she could only gape at him, the idea of him bungee jumping startling.

"Yeah, well, I hope you're a little smarter now."

The Jeep crawled like a snowplow up the drive of McKenzie's home. Matt parked his vehicle as close to the garage as possible. Before he could cut off the engine and respond, Valerie opened the door and jumped out. She trudged to the safety of the house through the pile of snow that had already fallen, running from the feelings Matt evoked. She liked Matt, but she was barely out of one disastrous relationship, and she wasn't about to bungee jump into another.

When she opened the door, the entryway was empty. She hurried up the stairs to her room. Soon, he would be gone, and in the meantime she would keep her distance. Sitting in the Jeep beside him tonight had stirred an aching sense of awareness of him as a man. If there had never been Carter, she would not have been able to resist the appeal she felt for Matt. But she'd be foolish to let down her guard after the recent events in her life.

Later, in her bedroom, she heard Matt's Jeep leave and she relaxed. She slipped into the flannel pajamas she'd recently bought and was just about to crawl in bed when the power flickered, and with a groan, disappeared. The house went completely dark, the silence deafening.

Carefully she made her way down the stairs to where McKenzie was lighting candles.

"Looks like we're going to have a long night ahead without power, which means no heat. I've got several sleeping bags, and I'm going to bunk down here in front of the fireplace. You're welcome to join me," McKenzie offered.

"What about the kids?"

"They're sound asleep. I put them in their bunny

pajamas and laid them together in my bed just in case this happened. I'll check on them later. They'll be fine upstairs under the down comforter I have on my bed."

"How long do you think we'll be without power?"

"Until the utility crews can reach us. At least until morning."

"I'm glad Matt was gone when it happened" Valerie quickly glanced at McKenzie. In the glow of candlelight she smiled.

"I thought you were getting along with my brother."

"I am. It's just that he's very determined."

"That's an understatement."

A flash of headlights and the sound of Matt's Jeep slugging through the snow as it slid into the driveway echoed in the room.

They both looked at each other and laughed. McKenzie said, "Sir Lancelot has returned."

A few minutes later they heard him in the mudroom, and then he entered the main room.

"Hey," he said, looking at them sheepishly in the candlelight. "I know why you don't have power. The storm blew a huge pine tree across the road, taking down power lines. The road is closed. Mind if I bunk in with you guys tonight?"

Even though he'd left with her bolting out of the car, she was glad he was here. His hair was ruffled and sprinkled with melting snow, yet he looked strong and manly in his coat and boots. Handsome enough she could feel her traitorous body responding.

McKenzie rose from the couch where she lay wrapped in her sleeping bag. "Sure, I'll get another sleeping bag."

"How about if I make some hot chocolate?" Valerie offered.

"That would be great. I'm frozen. I was afraid the Jeep was going to get stuck when I had to turn around."

Valerie stood and realized she wore her flannel pajamas and nothing else. Of course they weren't see-through or even tempting sexually. She'd bought them at the local discount store and paid a fourth of what her other nightwear cost. They were warm, comfortable, reliant, and nondescript and she loved them.

She strolled into the kitchen and placed a kettle of hot water on the stove. Thank God they still had gas. From the kitchen she watched Matt saunter to the fire and throw another log onto the blaze. He poked at the embers to stir the flames.

An uneasy silence filled the room.

"You must have lost power right after I left," he said.

"You weren't gone long."

"What about the kids? Is McKenzie going to move them in here with us?"

"No. She said they were asleep under the down comforter on her bed. She didn't want to disturb them."

McKenzie came down the stairs carrying two more sleeping bags and a box. "You're not going to believe what I found upstairs earlier today."

"Hopefully it didn't have four legs," Matt said.

"Very funny. Of course not. I found the box of pictures from when we were kids." She dropped the box on the table and lifted out a stack of fading photos. "We can show Valerie pictures of us when we were children."

"I'm sure she really wants to see a couple of nerdy kids."

"Hey, speak for yourself. I never looked like a nerd," McKenzie retorted.

"No, you were all legs and braces."

McKenzie threw the sleeping bag at her brother, hitting him squarely on the chest.

"Ooh, that gave me chest pains."

"Let me see if I can find that picture of you that Mother

took when you dressed like a girl."

"It was for Halloween," he exclaimed.

Valerie laughed at their antics and couldn't help but wonder, was this what it was like to have a sibling? As an only child she missed having someone to remember past times with. Someone who shared a bond to be close to.

"Ooh, here it is." McKenzie stared at the picture for a moment. "Hey, this isn't a Halloween picture. This was when you got into Mom's makeup."

"Give me that picture," Matt said, reaching for the photo in McKenzie's hand. "I was four years old."

She sidestepped away. "You know, I should send this to the paper for your birthday."

"You do and I will buy a billboard and put some hideous picture of you on it with the caption 'Call for a good time.'"

McKenzie raised her brows at her brother. "I'm not buying it, Mr. Overprotective."

She slipped the picture to Valerie, who ran to the stove, where at least a little light came off the flame. A mischievous little boy grinned at the camera, showing off his lipstick. He was a cute little tyke.

"Somehow fire-engine red isn't your color. And your technique with the lip brush needs some work. I know a makeup artist who could give you some pointers," Valerie told him, her voice teasing as she laughed at the picture.

He sneaked up behind her and reached for the photo. But she darted away, and he gave chase. As she dashed through the living room, she could hear him almost on her heels and felt a rush of adrenaline. What would it feel like if he caught her? Would he take her in his arms, hold her, kiss her?

The memory of his lips on hers was enough to cause her heartbeat to accelerate.

"I'd tackle you, but I'd probably crush you," he said,

his breathing heavy and close.

As she raced back into the kitchen, her socks slipped on the floor, and she felt herself falling. Suddenly his arms were around her, and he pulled her back against his solid chest, saving her from slamming onto the tile.

Her breathing stopped. Now she knew the feel of his arms around her, her back pressed against his chest, his lips close to her ear. He felt good, very good.

She glanced at him. "Good save."

He raised his brows. "Where's my picture?"

"Oh, now it's your picture." Valerie held up her hands, to show they were empty. "I don't have it."

"You didn't drop it. I was watching."

She shrugged, noncommittal.

"So that means it's still on your person."

Her lips curved up in anticipation.

He leaned in close to her ear, sending a shiver down her spine. "And that means I'm going to have to frisk you."

"I don't think so."

His arms were around her. She could feel his breath against her ear as she tried to control her own breathing. The strength and solidness of his chest was against her back. Being in his arms felt natural and good. She told herself it could be that way with any man.

But it hadn't been with Carter. The realization stunned her.

He placed his hand on her waist, his fingers warm and strong, and she had to resist the urge to lean into him. "There's only one place you could have hidden that picture."

"Put your hand inside my pajamas and you will pull back a bloody nub, bucko."

"Give me my photo and my hands will stay put," he answered, teasing, yet serious.

She tried to twist out of his grip but found his arms

strong and his hands firm, sending her blood pumping.

"I don't have your picture," she lied.

"Okay, I'm going to search until I find my photo." His right hand released her arm, while his left hand gripped her even harder. He moved his hand to the waistband of her pants.

A spark of excitement shivered down her spine at the feel of his hand against her flesh. His finger slowly traced the inside waistband of her pajama pants. Her breath suddenly clogged her throat. She glanced at him, and his gaze was dark, his breathing shallow.

That same spark of desire that burned her reflected from his emerald eyes, touching her in hidden areas, leaving behind a trail of fire.

He finished tracing the rim of her pants, and she knew her legs would soon buckle. Yet on the outside she appeared calm while her insides slowly melted. "The picture wasn't there. So you have to cook breakfast in the morning."

"Breakfast will be easy. Letting you go, hard," he said softly into her ear.

She swallowed. She'd wanted his hand to go farther. Yet his sister stood with her back to them, digging through the pictures. How could she be so attracted to this man? And why did she just now realize that there had never been a spark like this with Carter? This was the first time she'd ever been so stimulated by just a look, a touch, or even a kiss.

The whistle on the kettle screamed its message just as McKenzie released a soft sob.

Matt freed Valerie and turned to his sister. "Sis, what's wrong?"

She held a photo in her hand. "It's John. Oh God, I miss him so much."

Valerie walked into the kitchen and turned off the

burner. The whistle sang a slow death. She poured the hot water into cups as she watched Matt comfort his sister. It was touching to see him put his arm around McKenzie's shoulder and pull her close to him. She showed the photo to Matt.

"You guys were so young in this photo. John was a great guy. I miss him too," Matt said, consoling McKenzie.

"Yeah, he was." McKenzie dried her eyes and glanced at Valerie. "I'm sorry. Normally it doesn't hit me this hard, but this picture brought back so many memories."

"It's okay. I think our hot chocolate is ready. Let's sit in front of the fire and keep warm."

They pulled the couch and the chair closer to the fire. McKenzie brought the box of pictures.

"Why don't we save those pictures until later," Matt suggested. "I'm not sure that you're ready to look at them."

McKenzie shook her head. "No, I want to go through the box. I think I'm going to make a photo album for the twins of their father." She reached over and patted Matt on the hand. "Thanks. But this is just another part of the grieving process. I'll be fine. Besides, there are pictures of us in here as kids with Mom and Dad."

"Don't remind me," he said reluctantly.

"You need to forgive Dad and let it go," McKenzie said. "It doesn't do any good for you to hate him. It's not going to change things."

"You're right. But it keeps me warm at night and reminds me of why I hate liars."

A tremor like a buzzing alarm clock rippled through Valerie. Matt hated liars because of his father. Right now she was nothing but one big lie.

"Sorry, Valerie. As you can see, my brother is a stubborn man. Let me find you a manly picture of him."

"I still want that photo returned to me."

Valerie nodded. "Once the lights are back on, I'm sure

the picture will turn up."

"You hid that picture somewhere in the kitchen."

"Nope." She laughed. "But it was close to my heart."

"So I should have gone up, not down."

"You should keep your hands to yourself," she responded.

"Maybe, but maybe not."

"Excuse me, but you guys are not alone," McKenzie said, staring at the two of them, shocked. "You've gone from almost killing one another to sexual innuendos. Do I need to go sleep with the kids?"

"Don't you dare," Valerie insisted. "We'll be good."

"Speak for yourself," Matt said.

She frowned at Matt, trying to warn him off, but he just smiled at her, and somehow she knew that McKenzie was right. A shift had occurred in their relationship. Even though she'd tried to avoid this attraction, it was speeding toward her faster than an avalanche. She was about to get buried by none other than Matt.

And a part of her didn't want to resist.

Chapter Eight

The sound of giggling seeped into Valerie's sleep-fogged brain, and she woke enough to realize she wasn't in her bed. She snuggled closer to the heat that radiated from a hard male body she'd curled around and luxuriated in the warmth. Sometime in the night she had stuck her leg out of her sleeping bag and thrown it over Matt's thigh, insinuating her body against the hard muscles of his back. Reveling in his body heat, she'd slept like a baby.

And now she had to extradite herself before he awoke and realized she was draped all over him.

With trepidation she tried to separate herself from Matt, but his hand reached out and grabbed her leg.

She opened her eyes and stared into twin sets of big brown curious eyes gazing in wonder at the two of them.

"Good morning," he said, his back still to her.

"Good morning," she responded as she tried to jerk her leg free of his grasp.

"Where are you going? That leg feels great right there," Matt said, his voice sleep filled.

She cleared her throat nervously. "Your niece and nephew have just arrived and are standing over us."

He let go of her, and the twin's restraint crumpled. They jumped on top of their uncle, not waiting for an invitation.

"Snow. See snow."

Matt rolled away from her and wrapped an arm around each child, dragging them onto the sleeping bag with him. "What are you two doing awake so early?"

"Matt!" Ashley cried.

"Snow," Austin told him.

"What are you kids doing?" McKenzie called from the top of the stairs. "I'm sorry, guys. I told them to let you sleep."

"Are they always this happy when they wake up in the morning?" Matt asked groggily.

"Snow," Austin repeated as he bounced on his uncle's stomach.

"They had twelve hours of sleep last night and are completely recharged."

"Can I have just a little of that energy?" Matt asked, glancing over at Valerie.

She watched him with the children, yet she felt a little embarrassed to have been caught snuggled against him.

He sat up, pulling Austin and Ashley with him, and smiled at her. "You snore."

"I do not." She rose up on her elbows to defend herself.

"Well, maybe snore is not the appropriate word. Maybe purr is better."

"You're a cover hog."

"The better to entice you to my warmth." A mischievous grin lit up the darkened stubble on his chin.

"But it was my sleeping bag," she insisted.

"Got you closer, didn't it?" he asked.

"Go play in the snow," she told him, acting put out with him, while knowing that was the best rest she'd had all week. Even on the hardened floor, snuggling up against his hard, warm body, she'd slept deeply. No nightmares, no dreams, just rest.

The twins tugged on his arms. "Okay, I'm going to go see the snow."

She sat up and glanced at the embers in the fireplace. They had spent the night stoking the fire, adding wood and trying to keep the house warm. Sometime in the early morning hours, McKenzie had gone upstairs to sleep with the children. Not long after, Valerie had fallen asleep.

This morning the air was frosty and cold enough for her to see her breath. She reached over and with practiced ease, stirred the embers in the fireplace and added a new log. The flames flared to life, and heat radiated from the fire.

Matt let the twins lead him to the windows.

"Snow."

"Yes, that's a lot of snow. We got at least three feet last night," he said, pointing out the icicles to the kids.

"And still no power." McKenzie walked down the stairs in her robe. "I'm going to start breakfast."

"Nope," Matt replied, turning from the window. "I promised to cook Valerie breakfast last night if I couldn't find my picture. It's still missing."

McKenzie stared in amazement and looked between the two of them. "You're still speaking. I was afraid to leave you two alone last night. I didn't know who would be the lone survivor."

"I'm sure you lost sleep over it."

"Not hardly," McKenzie replied, getting out a pan for her brother. She glanced over at Valerie. "One of the reasons I like you is because you can hold your own with my big brother."

"Hey, did you think that maybe I need protecting?" Matt asked, indignant as he carried the children away from the window. "She could have ravished me in my sleep."

Valerie rolled her eyes. "In your dreams."

"Well, you did throw your leg over me."

"The act of a sleep-deprived woman seeking warmth."

"Oh, I see how it is. You used me for my body heat, and now this morning it's over. We're finished, and I didn't even get an 'it was good for me; was it good for you?' speech."

Valerie tipped her chin in his direction and cocked a brow. "The warmth was great, but you're right. *It's* over."

Even with the lack of sleep, Valerie felt saucy this morning. The night had been fun, but this morning she needed to put distance between her and Matt. There was an attraction there and she couldn't pursue it. Slowly she began to roll up the sleeping bags.

"Wanna play," Austin declared, tugging on his uncle's hand and pointing outside. Matt glanced at the toddler. "After breakfast, sport. Then we'll see about building a snowman."

Austin looked at him, a questioning expression on his young face.

"Trust me buddy, it will be fun. But first let me cook some smiley-face pancakes."

Matt kept the kids entertained with a pancake shuffle while he cooked their breakfast. He tossed the pancakes into the air, catching them with a plate. The twins giggled and then picked the blueberries from their pancakes to show their uncle they'd found the hidden treasure.

It took well over an hour for breakfast to be completed, and Valerie enjoyed watching the interaction between Matt and the twins. If she were looking for a husband, a good father, she had no doubt he would be the perfect catch.

But she wasn't in the market for a man and definitely not a husband. Though sleeping next to him last night had put her erogenous zones on high alert. Matt was a temptation she didn't need.

It took another thirty minutes to bundle the twins in their snowsuits and for everyone to gather at the door.

The first step into the freezing temperatures gave Valerie a moment's pause. It was colder than a well digger in Montana.

For a brief moment, the cold seemed to freeze the air in her lungs as she adjusted to cold. The sun shone brightly, but with the temperature hovering in the upper twenties, the snowy reflection of ice crystals showed no signs of melting. The outing would last until her fingers went numb.

"Come on, Austin, help me make the snowman," Matt said, leading the toddler into the fresh powder.

Valerie watched as Matt showed Austin how to roll the

snow into a big ball. Soon he had the little guy rolling a ball almost the same size as him around the yard. McKenzie and Ashley were busy making snow angels while Valerie gathered sticks for the arms of their snowman. She snuck a peak at Matt.

He was so patient with his nephew that it almost made her heart ache. Of all the lawyers she'd known, none of them played like Matt. None of them were as patient and kind, and none of them made her realize what she'd missed growing up an only child.

Someone seeing them for the first time might have assumed that Austin and Ashley were Matt's children. He couldn't take the place of his brother-in-law, but he had helped McKenzie create a family atmosphere for her children. A safe, warm, and loving home to nurture these little people into competent, happy adults.

The kind of place that Valerie could not remember ever having experienced in her life. An atmosphere she hoped to recreate with a man as good as Matt when she was ready to reconsider marriage.

"Hey," Matt called, throwing a snowball and hitting her squarely in the chest.

With a splat, a shower of cold snow snapped her out of her thoughts. Matt laughed and she whirled around, marching toward the house.

"Hey," he called.

She heard him running after her and knew he thought she was upset. Snow lay piled on the railing of the porch, and she hurried toward the fresh powder. When he was almost upon her, she scooped a handful of snow, turned, and splattered him.

"Hey, yourself," she said, watching him sputter as the snowball hit him smack in the lips.

He wiped the snow off his face. "You did that deliberately, didn't you?"

"Of course."

"It's war," he cried, reaching down to scoop up a handful of snow, pack it, and hurl the frozen ball at her.

She ran, but the snow hit her in the back. He machine-gunned her with snowballs, pelting her as fast as she ran. She took cover behind his completed snowman, knowing he wouldn't destroy Austin's first attempt.

"Hey, you two, I'm taking the kids in the house. They're getting cold," McKenzie called.

Neither of them moved or acknowledged her. Valerie heard him approach the snowman. She peeked out from behind the ice creature only to find herself being lifted in his arms.

"Put me down."

"No problem!"

He dropped her onto the snow and proceeded to cover her with the loose powder. She dragged him down with her, and the two of them rolled together, stuffing snow in any available opening, laughing and squealing.

The ice slithered down the front of her coat, causing her to shriek with glee and shiver, though not from the cold.

Her body tingled, hot with desire that should have had the snow vaporizing.

She landed on top of him. While he tried to put more snow down the inside of her jacket, she yanked the zipper down on his coat and pushed some inside his shirt. Her glove connected with his bare chest, and she plastered him, wiping the grin from his face.

"Agh, that's cold." His voice seemed strangely tense as he stared at her, his pupils dilated, his breathing heavy, and his eyes exuding sultry warmth. She stopped her fist in midair as his gaze melted the ice from her heart.

Though the temperature outside was cold, inside, her body thermometer spiked. She lay on top of him, her hipbone to his, her thighbone connected to his, her breasts against his chest. Her breath shallow and fast.

"Do you dare go lower with that snowball?" he taunted, glancing briefly at the snow in her hand.

"Maybe I should cool you off with it?" she responded, her voice deeper and breathy.

"That little snowball doesn't stand a chance. You're going to need a whole platoon of snowmen."

She could feel his erection beneath her, and that both frightened and excited her. Though Valerie wanted to deny her reaction, she knew her breathing gave her away. Yes, she was so hot for him that she feared getting burned. How had she let herself get in such a precarious position?

"We better go in," she said, feeling the urge to run.

His hand reached up and brushed a lock of her hair away from her face, the tender action almost her undoing.

"Yeah, I guess you're right. It's either go in or have sex right here in the front yard. I don't think my sister would approve, and since her neighbors are my clients, I guess we'd better think of somewhere else to have sex."

What was she doing? Nothing about her situation had changed, and by being with Matt, she was playing with fire. He was talking about sex like it was inevitable.

She knew he was half-serious, half-teasing, but it reminded her of all the reasons why they could never be together. They could never kiss again. They could never have sex.

"Think again." She pushed off him and rose from the ground. "Sex is out of the question."

Without looking back, she strode into the house, dusting snow off her as she went.

<u>Focus, Valerie.</u> The goal is to leave Springtown, not find a lover. It didn't matter that Matt left her hot and needy. It didn't matter that her body craved his. No men. No lovers. No Matt.

~

Two days later, Matt couldn't help but remember the morning he had awoken with Valerie snuggled beside him. The feel of her body nestled against his, her leg intimately thrown over his own, had brought forth a hunger in him that food could never quench.

Not to mention she could make flannel pajamas look like a Victoria's Secret commercial.

That morning he'd been awake listening to the sound of her breathing, enjoying the feel of her body, the weight of her leg thrown over him.

Sometimes he saw such wistfulness in her eyes that he wondered at the source. Flirty and receptive one moment, she could turn colder than a blizzard in a nanosecond. Like the click of a switch, she could turn off and on the charm with an ease that had him flip-flopping worse than a politician.

So much so that he wondered if that was the reason why he still didn't believe she'd told him everything about herself. For the moment, he was willing to wait, to give her the opportunity to tell him why she resisted this attraction between them. Why she'd arrived in Springtown on a bus.

Today would be the first time he'd seen her since they awoke in each other's arms and spent the day playing in the snow until the subject of sex came up. Then she'd bolted like a scared doe in hunting season.

Still, he was anxious to see her. He wanted to hold her, kiss her, and tell her whatever troubled her they would resolve together. But for now, he waited impatiently.

The outside door opened.

"It's just me," she called.

Unable to stop himself, he hurried to greet her. "Hey, how are you?"

"I'm great. How about yourself?"

"Good. I see you survived our worst snowstorm in three years," he said, standing in front of her, his arms crossed over his chest. God, he wanted to fidget so badly, but he refused to let his nervousness show.

"Yes," she said, her answer short and succinct. "How much work do you have for me today?"

Once again the walls between them were resurrected, and he hated having to scale them every time they came together. The all-work Valerie stood before him, and he so wanted the teasing, playful girl to return. He wanted the girl who had relaxed enough to let the walls she'd erected come down. He wanted the sexy, soft, pliant Valerie.

"Not much. You took good care of things while I was gone, and well, until I hear from Denver, we're kind of slow."

"Even the café is slow."

"Let's take the day off and go skiing," he offered, so wanting them to have fun again.

"No, I don't think so. I'll just see if I can catch a ride to McKenzie's."

"What do you mean, catch a ride?"

"Well, I don't have transportation of my own, so I think that means either walk or hitchhike."

The thought of her hitchhiking was frightening. "No, let me get my coat. I have to run an errand, and I'll take you home after I'm done."

"Where is this errand?" she asked, fidgeting.

"We're just dropping off some paint on the way to McKenzie's."

"Okay." She slipped her coat back on.

Matt grabbed his coat, hat, and gloves, and they strode out of the office. The temperature hovered below freezing, and the snow glittered in the bright sunshine.

Valerie climbed into his Jeep. "Are you sure you don't mind driving me home?"

He shrugged. "Not at all."

Matt started the car. His frustration and disappointment at her attitude overcame him, and he deliberately goaded her. "You're acting weird. Is it because we spent the night together? Do you always act this way with a new man in your life?"

She turned on him, her blue eyes sparking with fire. "First of all, we did not *spend the night together,* and second, you are not the new man in my life."

He grinned. It was almost too easy to get a rise out of her. He turned the car onto the highway that led out of town.

"You did that on purpose, didn't you?" she demanded a few minutes later.

"But I could be the new man in your life." He spoke the words in a teasing way, although he was completely serious. His attempt to keep the situation light and funny wasn't working.

"Before you make that kind of statement, you should talk to the last man in my life. You might want to reconsider."

Matt took his eyes from the road. "Why? What did you do to him? Break his heart?"

"No, nothing quite so simple."

"Hmmm, take his money?"

"Hardly," she responded.

He raised his eyebrows in mock surprise. "Oh no, you didn't!"

She stared at him, perplexed. "What?"

"Tied him up and left him!"

"I wasn't given the opportunity, or I might have considered that one."

He chuckled. "So are you going to tell me?"

She paused a moment, toying with him the way he had toyed with her earlier, capturing his interest and holding him hostage.

"Nope. I'm not going to tell you. I just wanted to plant a seed and let your mind germinate for a while."

"Sounds kinky."

"Hardly."

Valerie frowned at him. "Matt, when I leave, you'll realize it was for the best we didn't get involved."

"Are you going somewhere?"

"Eventually, I will leave town."

"Unless I convince you to stay. I'm a determined man. I'm not giving up."

"You can say that again. You know you were easier to control when you were trying to run me out of town."

Matt paused for a moment and considered her. "Control. That's an interesting word choice."

She gave him a smile. "The word completely turns off some people. Especially when you use it concerning them."

She was trying to rile him into backing off. "Yes, it does. Fortunately, I'm not one of those people.

He turned off the main highway and traveled an unplowed road. He put the Jeep in four-wheel drive.

"We're not going to get stuck are we?"

"We could, but I never have yet."

The road began a gradual ascent up the mountain. He watched as she gripped the armrest.

"Relax, it's safe."

"I'm perfectly fine," she said, leaning as far back as her seat allowed.

"Well, you're leaving fingernail marks in the leather of the armrest."

She yanked her hand up, and he laughed as fingernail indentions slowly unfurled.

They topped the mountain, and a white meadow filled with pine trees and aspens came into view. Matt stopped the car in front of his half-finished log home.

"Whose house is this?"

"Mine." He switched off the Jeep, and for a moment they stared at the cabin.

"Very impressive," she commented.

"Thanks. The outside work is done, but the inside is not complete yet. Most of the contractors work for the county in the winter and drive the snowplows part-time. I just hope they're finished by spring."

He opened the car door and lifted the paint cans from the back. "Come on and let me show you the place while I drop off this paint."

Before he could come around and help her, Valerie opened her door and jumped out.

They strode up the wooden front steps and across the porch. The wind whispered through the pines, a gentle, yet cold breeze with the trees showering fallen snow from their branches. Opening the door, they walked into a foyer area that stepped down into a sunken room with a huge rock fireplace. He set the paint cans down just inside the door.

"Oh my, this is beautiful." Valerie strolled around the room admiring the spacious living area that opened to the kitchen. She wandered through the kitchen and returned to the front room. "This will be a great for entertaining guests. What's upstairs?"

"My office, the master bedroom, and three other bedrooms."

"Seems like a lot of space for just you."

"For now," he commented. "Someday I would like to get married and have a half-dozen kids."

"Half a dozen?"

"Well, I'm open to discussion on the number."

"I'm sure the woman you marry will be glad to hear that. Show me your office?" she asked, changing the subject.

Why was it whenever he told her anything serious, she

abruptly changed the subject? He'd planned on bringing her here eventually, when he felt more certain they had a chance at being a couple.

He wanted to see her reaction to the house he was building. It was a test to see if there was a possibility of anything between the two of them working. He'd kissed her, he'd slept next to her, he knew they had fun together, and they had this awesome attraction. But before he made a complete fool of himself, he wanted to judge her reaction to living in the middle of God's country.

He followed her up the stairs. When they reached his office, he opened the door for her. Windows along the west wall gave a gorgeous view of the Rocky Mountains. The room was big enough for a large desk, and built-in bookshelves lined one wall.

"Wow," she said as she strolled into the room, her footsteps echoing on the bare floors. "This is nothing like your office in town."

"Do you like it?"

"The view alone is fantastic, and the room has some great possibilities."

"If you like this view, come see the master bedroom."

Valerie gave him a cautious look, but he took hold of her hand and pulled her down the hall to the bedroom.

She gasped when she strolled into the room. The east wall of the huge room was nothing but floor to ceiling windows. "You can lie in bed and look out at the mountains."

He grinned. "I wanted to watch the sun rise over the Rockies every morning and the moon rise at night."

"You'll certainly be an early riser, unless you buy some heavy-duty drapes."

"No drapes."

She gazed at him her face astonished. "You're serious about settling here."

"I'm never returning to work permanently in Denver. I want to move my law practice here full-time and only go to Denver when I have no choice."

He drew her into his arms, and the look in her eyes became both responsive and wary at the same time. "I like you, Valerie. I have fun with you, and there is something between us that I want to explore further."

"Matt—"

"Shh, don't spoil this moment. Just go with it for once. Let yourself feel."

Matt pulled her tight against him and his lips covered hers. At first she remained stiff, but then slowly she relaxed in his arms, her body going soft against him. She tasted sweet, tempting, and his hands pressed her hard against his erection. For weeks, he'd wanted her. If only he could lay her on the unfinished wood floor and show her the passion that ignited between the two of them.

How could she deny they could be a great couple when she experienced the fire between them? How could she ignore the desire they generated together?

She pulled back and stared at him, her eyes brimming with smoky sensuality. He could see her resisting, but her response to his kiss was proof this wasn't just a one-sided affair.

"What is it you think we have?" she asked, her voice low and breathless.

His lips layered over hers. He didn't want to hear her say that they had nothing, because as much as she denied the electrical current that connected them, it was there, igniting a firestorm of passion. He covered her lips with his mouth, pressing her breasts against his chest. His hands held her head in his, tilting her mouth to the angle that he needed. She moaned beneath his touch, and he knew she felt this magnetism too.

Her arms reluctantly came up and wrapped around him,

and she clung to him.

More than he needed his next breath, he needed to feel her flesh. He slid his hand beneath her coat and sweater, pushed her bra away, and eagerly sought her breast. His hand cupped her, her flesh soft as silk as he kneaded her nipple until it beaded beneath his fingers. She moaned deep in her throat. He wasn't ready to promise her forever, but he was willing to at least investigate tomorrow.

He knew he had to stop now, before he lost control. His mouth released hers, his breathing harsh.

"Valerie, we're good together. Good enough that I'm serious when I say that I want to explore if something more meaningful could happen between us."

She stiffened in his arms and jerked away, breaking the spell. She stepped back, putting distance between them.

"I'm ready to settle down and have stability, a family. Put down roots. We work well together, and there's passion between us."

Matt watched her, not saying a word, wondering what he'd done wrong.

Her eyes were wide and wary as she returned his stare. Her breathing fast, shallow, her eyes dilated. She was affected by this attraction just as much as he was.

"What is it you want from me?" she asked, her voice rising in the empty room. "Do you want to hear me say I'm attracted to you? Will that satisfy you? Fine, I'm very attracted to you. But there are so many reasons why we can't get involved."

"Like what? Tell me."

Valerie folded her arms across her chest and faced him. "We don't know each other."

"All I'm asking is a chance to get to know one another."

She dropped her arms and began to pace the room. "You don't understand. I didn't come here to get involved with a man."

"Involvement wasn't on my agenda either."

"You're a lawyer!" she cried.

"What has that got to do with anything?" he asked in shock.

"I'm not any good at relationships."

"You're not even willing to give us a chance."

"It won't work." She stopped pacing and faced him. "Let's just have sex, no commitments, no tomorrows. Just one night of hot sex to satisfy this attraction we feel."

The image of the two of them locked naked in each other's arms sent a flash of sexual heat and temptation through him. Shocked, he stared at her, trying to control the frustration he knew would not serve him well. He considered what she was offering. It could be a chance to bring them closer, or it could be a crushing blow to his ego.

Part of him wanted to jump at the opportunity she offered, but he was sick of just sex. He wanted, no he needed, more. He could get just sex anywhere.

He wanted a chance at a committed relationship, and she wanted quick meaningless sex.

"Not just sex," he finally said, his growing anger and hurt under wraps.

She swallowed and placed her hand at her throat. "I'm not looking for a committed relationship."

His breathing was heavy, his loins tight with need, his pride smarting, and he did the hardest thing he'd ever done in his life. "And I'm not looking to just hook up."

"Too bad," she said a little too eagerly for his liking.

For a moment he stared at her and realized she was willing to walk away. That insight left him frustrated. He wanted a chance at a relationship, and she wanted sex before moving on.

Without a word he strode from the room and down the stairs. Anger radiated through him. He needed to get away before he said something he regretted. Part of him wanted to rage at her, at the possibility of what she was throwing away, yet the rational part knew he needed to simply walk.

He opened the outside door and went straight to the car. He climbed in the Jeep and started the engine.

In a few moments she stormed out of the house, slamming the door behind her. Quickly she climbed into the car.

"I'll take you to McKenzie's," he said quietly, and turned the car from the house of his dreams.

He wouldn't settle for just a hookup with this woman when he wanted more, so much more.

If he couldn't have it all, then he'd probably just thrown away his only chance of having sex with Valerie.

That thought really bummed him. But he wanted something more from her than just scratching an itch.

Chapter Nine

A week later, Matt drove the Jeep, his brain on autopilot as he mulled over the dilemma with Valerie. Frustration gripped him like a fist about his throat. How many women would settle for just a hookup?

Today while Valerie worked at the café, he would visit McKenzie and get her opinion on the bizarre way Valerie had responded. In the past week he had avoided his own office and the café. He had even taken a trip to Denver to put some distance between him and the blonde who had gotten under his skin. Anywhere, while his anger simmered and cooled.

It disturbed him that he'd finally found someone who intrigued him, someone he wanted to explore a relationship with, and every time he made a move, she threw up a roadblock. If the attraction wasn't mutual, he would have walked away, but she responded to him. Whenever he touched her, passion reflected from her blue eyes, and she quivered in his arms. Clearly she was caught off guard by the attraction, yet she refused to acknowledge the magnetism simmering between them.

And frankly, that pissed him off.

The Jeep came to a halt in front of his sister's log home. He watched McKenzie and the twins playing outside in the cold sunshine. Bundled in their winter jumpers, the kids waddled around like fat little penguins.

McKenzie chased the toddlers through the snow, tossing a snowball at them. Ashley and Austin squealed with laughter, and Matt felt sad that his brother-in-law was not here to witness his children's giggles.

John's death had been tough on his sister, yet Matt envied her life. Not the death of her husband, but the love he'd witnessed between them and now the twins.

Clearly John's death had shown Matt that life was

short, and he wanted to experience a lasting love with a family of his own.

Not the marriage of his parents, in which deception, lies, and hate permeated the relationship like a cancer until its death.

The single lifestyle had left him with enough cell numbers to fill a phone book, more boring dates than he cared to remember, and an ever-present loneliness. He didn't want his bed to be a revolving door of meaningless hookups. He longed for a woman who'd stay through the good times and the bad. A best friend and a lover. A love that lasted beyond the next morning. And it all began with Valerie giving them the opportunity to explore this attraction.

All he wanted was a chance to see if this fascination was something they could build on.

He jumped out of the Jeep, and his sister turned around and waved. "Hey you, come in and have some hot chocolate."

"Sure," he said as he ran through the snow toward the twins.

"Uncle Matt!" Ashley cried, hurrying toward him, her short little legs stumbling in the deep snow.

He picked her up and twirled her in the air. She screamed with delight.

"Me too, Uncle Matt. Me too," Austin cried, wrapping his arms around Matt's leg.

He set Ashley down, picked-up Austin and twirled him.

"More," Austin cried when his feet connected with the ground. "More."

Matt's heart filled with love for these two little ones. Maybe he would never have a family of his own. Yet he wasn't ready to concede on finding that special person, even if she wasn't Valerie.

"Come on," he said, taking them each by the hand.

"Let's go have hot chocolate."

"But I want to stay outside and play," Austin whined, puckering his mouth in a pout.

Ashley stuck out her lower lip, mimicking her brother.

"Hey, don't stick out your lips. They might freeze that way."

McKenzie gave her twins a stern motherly look, her eyebrows raised. "Come on you two, it's been an hour. I told you we couldn't stay out long. Besides we have cookies waiting for us inside."

The twins let go of his hand and raced toward their mother.

"Bribery gets them every time," she admitted to Matt.

They piled into the mudroom, discarding their coats and boots. Slipped on their house slippers and ran to their toys, their mother, Matt, and the cookie forgotten.

"Are they always that easy?"

"Oh no, it becomes more of a challenge every day. I've learned it's best to switch their attention to something else. It creates fewer tantrums."

Matt slipped out of his coat and hung it on a hook, suddenly reminded of everything his sister did for her children, alone. She never got a break.

"Are you doing okay?" he asked as they walked into the kitchen.

Concern creased her forehead and reflected from her eyes. "Yes, I'm fine."

"I worry about you being alone and taking care of the kids. You never get a break."

"Their naptime is my time. It's hard, but I'm okay."

He wondered how much she wasn't telling him. "I know you miss John."

She sighed, the sound loud in the room. "Every day." She picked up the kettle, ran hot water into it, and then placed it on the stove. "But what about you? You're acting kind of strange. Not my typical all confidant, devil-may-care brother. What's wrong?"

He laughed, the sound sarcastic as he took a seat at the table. "You know me too well."

"Well, you're acting strange, and Valerie has been withdrawn these last few days. Something going on that I need to know about?"

He couldn't help but feel a little glad to hear that Valerie wasn't her normal cheerful self. He wanted to tell his sister his side. He needed a woman's interpretation of Valerie's reaction. "She only wants a hookup."

"A what?" McKenzie said, stunned.

"Valerie. She said she didn't want commitment."

"Did she specifically say she wanted a one night stand?" McKenzie questioned, her voice uncertain.

His mind replayed their conversation. He'd been so shocked and angry that his skills as a lawyer hadn't kicked in until he'd made it to his car. The last time he'd been that angry was when John died.

"Tell me what she said."

"Her exact words were 'let's have one night of hot sex, no commitments, no tomorrows,'" he blurted out, the anger spiking as he clenched his fists. "I wanted her to at least give this attraction between us a chance."

"Okay, I feel very lost. How did you guys get on the subject of sex, and why did you say no?"

He rubbed his hand over his face, the rough texture a comfort as he told his sister the conversation, ending with his realization. "When I made her face that we were attracted to one another, she asked me if I wanted sex. I don't want just sex."

"What did she say after you said no?" McKenzie questioned.

"Her response was I don't want a commitment, and I said I didn't want to just hook up." He shook his head. "To which she responded, 'too bad.'"

Silence hung heavy between them. The children sat in the corner playing with blocks while his sister sat contemplating, making him nervous. McKenzie glanced at Austin and Ashley and back at Matt.

He couldn't restrain himself. "We have this chemistry, and she refuses to acknowledge that we're attracted to one another. She won't even give us a chance."

"And you assumed she just wanted a…what did you call it? A hookup, because she said 'too bad'?"

"Well, when you're in the moment and she tells you she's not interested in a committed relationship, what else am I supposed to think?" His voice rose. "Most women would like the fact that the guy doesn't want just a quick lay. Most women would be excited that the guy was thinking relationship. A connection that could become more than just sex."

McKenzie stared at him, knowingly. "And you got angry."

"Hell, yes. I'm still angry. I know what I want, and she's the first woman I've met in two years that was worth considering."

McKenzie began to laugh softly.

"What is so funny?" he asked, frustrated.

"First you wanted to run her out of town, and now you can't wait to get into her pants."

"I…I… That's not exactly true."

"Oh? Who didn't want her moving in here with me?"

"Well, I didn't."

"Who wanted Jesse to run a background check on her?" McKenzie asked.

"How did you know about that?"

"You're my brother. You're a lawyer. You did, didn't you?" she questioned.

"Well, yes."

"And you found nothing."

"No."

The whistle on the teakettle squealed, and McKenzie rose. She poured them both a cup of hot, steaming chocolate and placed a cup in front of him.

She sipped from her cup and said softly, "Valerie hasn't told me what brought her here, but I know that first night, she seemed to be in shock. Now, the longer she's here the more she seems to open up. But at first she appeared spooked, almost afraid."

"My thoughts exactly, but everyone got mad at me for trying to investigate her," Matt said with annoyance in his voice.

He sipped from his cup, willing his anger back while the hot liquid soothed him.

McKenzie nodded. "That's because sometimes you approach obstacles in life with such determination that you mow over anyone who gets in your way. If you could just ease back the throttle a little, you could learn the truth." She sipped her chocolate. "You put people off with that single-minded resolve."

"It's what I do for a living."

She laughed. "I can see that. It's probably what makes you so good in the courtroom."

"But not in personal relationships," he admitted.

She nodded slowly. "Sometimes you are too overpowering. I think someone hurt Valerie. You need to back off and give her time. If the two of you are meant to be, it will happen in her time frame. And if you don't like that, well, I can tell you she'll soon be on a bus out of town."

"Damn it, McKenzie. *That's not what I wanted to hear.*"

McKenzie smiled. "Sorry, I'm not here to sugarcoat life and only say what you want to hear. I'm going to tell you how I see it."

Matt hung his head. "I didn't expect to think of her this way. When I first saw her come into the café, I thought she was beautiful, but not my type. But soon she was everywhere. And it isn't just her looks that attracted me. She doesn't back down. She isn't afraid to stand up to me. At first I thought she wasn't very smart, but I was so wrong. Her mind is quick and sharp. She has my office running better than any office I've worked in. And I like her. I like being with her."

McKenzie reached out, took Matt's hand, and squeezed it. "Back off and give her some time. Let her deal with whatever is haunting her."

"Has she told you what brought her to Colorado?"

"Nope, and I know better than to ask," McKenzie said. "When she's ready, she'll tell all of us. But until then give her some space."

Matt drained his hot chocolate. "You women stick together. You've only made me more curious about who she is. But I will try to wait for her."

"You better, or you'll lose her."

"Well, you haven't exactly cheered me."

"Hey, if she's as good as you think she is, then she's worth waiting for."

"Yeah, I know. But I don't have much patience. Especially when I want something."

McKenzie smiled but didn't say a word.

"Thanks for listening to me."

"Not a problem. Come by anytime."

"Yeah, and when you think you're about to go nuts, call me. I'll watch the kids for you," he promised.

"I will take you up on that very soon."

He stood, and McKenzie rose and followed him to the mudroom. He grabbed his coat and muffler and put them on.

Impulsively, he hugged McKenzie. "Thanks, sis."

"You're welcome. Just remember, I think she's worth waiting for too."

~

Valerie stared gloomily out the café window. She'd read the paper, filled the salt and pepper shakers, scrubbed every table, swept the floor, and even dusted the windowsills. She was bored out of her mind and sat contemplating mopping the floors.

Fran sank onto the chair across from her. "If you clean one more thing, I'm going to send you to my house."

"I'm bored."

"Bored? The way you scoured the tables and chairs, it looked more like you were erasing some memory," Fran declared. "You know, when I was married, anytime I got angry with my husband, my house would shine. I scoured the very scent of that man away. Should I get the mop?"

Valerie frowned at the nosy waitress. "I'm not mad. I'm okay."

"If this is what you call okay, you need to call Dr. Phil and see if you can make an appointment." Fran's eyes grew large, and she raised her brows. "That was supposed to be a joke."

"It wasn't funny."

"Yeah, well, I was trying to put a smile on that pretty face. You keep scowling and you'll soon need a face-lift."

"I don't need cheering. I'm just bored."

Fran sighed, her fingers drumming the table as she looked inquiringly at Valerie. "I haven't seen Matt in here for a couple of days."

"So."

"You guys have your first fight?"

"We are not a couple! And no we didn't have a fight."

"Good. I was afraid you would walk in here one day

and tell me you were quitting to work for him full-time."

"You don't have to worry. I'm sure he'll fire me any day."

The older woman frowned at her. "What makes you think that? Matt told me his office was running like a well-oiled machine since you'd come to work for him."

Valerie was tired of hiding from her problems, and she felt just mean enough to want to shock Fran. "That was before I asked him to have sex with me."

A shocked silence came between the two women before Fran began to laugh.

"What is so funny? I don't find the situation amusing at all."

"Matt turned you down?"

"What man alive would turn down no-strings sex?" Valerie asked, indignation in her voice.

"He's not attracted to you?"

"Oh, believe me, there is enough mutual attraction to heat Palooka County all winter," Valerie admitted. "It's just that…"

Fran sat back, shook her head and grinned.

"He didn't want just a hookup. Oh nooooo, he wants a relationship." She slammed her hand on the table. "It's the twenty-first century! Sometimes people just have sex!"

"Well, honey, most women want more."

"Not me!" Valerie leaned back and crossed her arms.

"Matt is a great guy. He's honest, hard-working. He's a decent man. And he sure ain't hard on the eyes." Fran gave her a stern look. "You're attracted to one another. The problem must be with you. So why are you trying to run him off? What are you afraid of?"

She frowned and knew that everything Fran said was true. The problem did lie with her. But how did she get over the fear of being involved with another man? This man she feared could hurt her way more than the last one.

She was still recovering from her life's unexpected turn, and yet here was Matt, a caring, hard-working man who stirred places in her heart she hadn't known existed. She wanted to have sex with Matt, but the thought was scary.

Fran watched her, waiting.

"You're right. It's me, Fran," Valerie confessed, not feeling any better. She toyed with a napkin full of silverware, needing something in her hands. "I'm afraid of saying yes and I'm afraid of saying no. Does that make any sense?"

"Oh, honey," she reached out to pat Valerie's hand.

"Matt wants commitment, and that word paralyzes me with fear. I can't think past today without needing to call 911."

"Is panic what put you on that bus to Denver?" Fran asked.

Valerie nodded, unable to speak.

"Oh, honey, you need to stop running and face whatever sent you over the edge. You'll be crippled with fear until you take care of whatever had you jumping on that bus."

Tears welled up in Valerie's eyes as she stared out the window, unable to face Fran. She couldn't tell her. She couldn't tell anyone what she was running from without revealing she'd lied. And that hurt almost as much as what Carter had done to her. She hated the fact that she had come here and lied about who she was to cover her tracks. These people had become her friends, her family, and she had deceived them.

Right now, she didn't like herself very much, but at the time, she'd believed she had no choice. And she still didn't have a choice unless she wanted her father and Carter sweeping into town.

But Fran did deserve to know the reason behind her

skipping town.

"My former fiancé…he did something that sent me running five minutes before I was to walk down the aisle. I'm afraid he's still looking for me. He can't find me, Fran."

"I don't know what to say, Valerie," Fran said quietly.

"I thought as much. We're your friends here. And if Matt cares about you, he'll give you time. Have you explained to him the reason why you only wanted to hook up?"

"No." She shrugged and wiped the tears from her eyes. "I was trying to shock him into going away. By offering him just a hookup, I took a big chance that he might have said yes."

Fran shook her head. "Well, honey, I'm sure that didn't sit too well with his male pride. You know a man like Matt has way too much testosterone and ego as it is. You need to explain your reaction to him."

"He's been avoiding me."

"I'm sure he has. He probably doesn't know what to think," She patted Valerie's arm. "So do you care about him?"

Valerie sighed. "More than I should."

"Then talk to him. Explain to him that you need some time. You aren't committing to a lifetime, just to seeing one another."

"That's what he wanted, and I couldn't even give him that much. I panicked."

And since that day, that small reasonable part of her brain had kept asking her what was she doing. What if her cowardice caused her to miss out on the best man she'd ever met? What would it hurt to just let things happen?

"You're right. I've been avoiding him," she admitted, not knowing how to explain to Matt that she wanted to explore their attraction but was so afraid.

"You've got to face Matt, and eventually you're going

to have to face the demons you're running from," Fran said in a comforting voice.

"I know. I'm just not ready. It's been peaceful here in Springtown. I'm not ready for the demons in my past to catch up to me and destroy the peace I've found here."

And how did she explain to Matt that she wasn't Valerie Brown, but Valerie Burrows? And she'd burned her fiancé's car.

~

Later that night, alone in the restaurant, Valerie swabbed the floor, her thoughts focused on how Matt would feel when she told him the truth. He obviously thought that being truthful was important, and she'd lied to him. Her entire life here in Springtown was a lie, yet she hadn't meant to fall in love with the little town. Life here was simpler, not the fast paced, society-focused existence her father insisted upon.

She could live like she wanted while not having the pressure of living up to her father's expectations. She wasn't an heiress apparent, but just a waitress.

But how would Matt react when he learned she'd lied? How would he respond when he learned her father was a top liability lawyer in Dallas?

What would he think when he learned she'd deliberately run from her own wedding? What would he think when he learned she was wanted for questioning by the police?

The piercing shrill of the smoke alarm caused her to drop the mop. The noise sent her heart racing into her throat. For the first time she noticed smoke pouring into the dining area.

Dear God, Fran had left her alone, and the kitchen was on fire.

Valarie ran to the kitchen. Going through the swinging

doors, smoke slammed into her face, and she gasped as the heat caused her to suck in the toxic air. She backed out of the kitchen, coughing, and yanked the phone from its cradle. Quickly she dialed 911.

"We have a fire at the Mountain Chalet Café. Send a truck."

"Ma'am are you in the building?" the operator asked.

"Yes," she said, choking on the smoke.

"Get out now!"

She dropped the phone, turned to run when she saw the fire extinguisher hanging on the wall. This was her friend Fran's restaurant. The woman who had befriended Valerie in her darkest hour. She yanked the extinguisher from the wall. With a deep breath, she plunged back into the smoke.

Flames roared from a pan of grease, licking at the ceiling tiles. If the tiles caught fire, the entire building would sizzle like a sparkler on the fourth of July.

Adrenaline and fear rocked through her, and she pushed the emotion aside. With a yank, she pulled the pin on the handle, aimed the nozzle at the base of the fire, and squeezed the trigger. In the distance she could hear sirens wailing and knew the fire department was on its way.

A steady stream of chemicals spewed onto the base of the flames as she held her aim steady. Smoke bellowed from the fire, making it almost impossible to see, the air dank with fumes and smoke. She coughed and tried to hold her breath and not breathe the toxic fumes.

A fireman burst into the kitchen, a hose in his hands. He yelled something, and a second fireman appeared before her eyes.

He took the empty extinguisher from her hands and led her through the smoky dining room and out the building. She could hear the firemen yelling to one another in the kitchen, the smoky scene surreal to her, almost like she was in a dream.

She stepped outside to see the red-and-white lights of the fire truck flashing their warning. The whine of the engine pump filled the cold night while she breathed the fresh air and coughed so hard she thought she would faint.

"Are you hurt?" the fireman asked.

"No," she gasped, her lungs burning, her throat scratchy as her mind began to clear.

"Take slow breaths. I'll have the paramedics check you out." He sat her down on the curb in the cold, but she didn't mind. The air was clean, and though it hurt to breath, she felt relief.

The fireman brought over a paramedic and then disappeared back into the building.

Police tape fluttered in the cold breeze, and Jesse stood watching the firemen, keeping onlookers back. His eyes widened at the sight of her and he hurried over. "Are you all right?"

She tried to talk but all she could do was cough.

A paramedic slipped an oxygen hose around her head and a cannula into her nose. "Try to breathe normally."

While the paramedic took her vital signs, all the tension and fear in her body overwhelmed her, and she began to shake. It was cold outside, but the cold she felt was from within. Fran had left her alone in the restaurant, and it almost burned to the ground.

Valerie had not left the pan of grease on, but she still felt responsible.

"Hey, you're okay. Don't be going into shock on me," the paramedic said as he placed a blanket over her shoulders. "Your vital signs are good. I'm only giving you oxygen to clear your lungs."

Fran pushed through the crowd, her face white and her eyes large and frightened. "Thank God! I was so worried when I saw the fire truck. Are you all right? What happened?"

Valerie nodded, her hands shaking. She tried to speak and her voice croaked. "Stove…"

Fran hugged her close, and Valerie savored her embrace. The person who had given her a job and found her shelter, when she needed it most, Valerie treasured Fran's friendship and would have done anything to save her friend's restaurant.

"I don't give a good crap about the restaurant. I have insurance."

Fran glanced at the paramedic for reassurance.

"She's fine. She breathed in some smoke, so we're taking preventive measures to make sure she's all right."

Valerie pushed back, needing to breathe the oxygen, trying to clear her fogged mind. Black streaks were smudged on Fran's clothes where their bodies had touched.

"Grease," Valerie choked out. "Pan."

Fran's eyes crinkled and her face grimaced. "I fried some french fries, but I thought I turned that fire off. Besides, Todd was still in the kitchen, and he always checks everything before he leaves."

"I was mopping…"

"It doesn't matter. No one was hurt and I was going to remodel the kitchen in the next six months. The remodeling will just start sooner."

The fireman came to the door, and Fran hurried over to him. "Can I go in?"

"Sure, the fire's out. We've shut off the gas, and now we're checking to make sure there are no hot spots."

Fran followed the fireman inside, leaving Valerie to sit and breathe in the clean air and calm her pounding heart. Her lungs ached and her head drummed like a marching band. She closed her eyes.

When she opened them several minutes later, Matt stood in front of her. Tears welled up in her eyes at the sight of him. She resisted the urge to throw her arms around him.

His gaze held hers, and without a word he shrugged out of his coat and wrapped it around her.

"Are you okay?" he asked quietly.

She nodded, afraid to speak. Her throat felt scratchy and rough, and her emotions clogged her throat. She refused to cry in front of him. She refused to let him see her vulnerable and weak.

"Water," she managed to croak, needing a diversion.

A few minutes later, Jesse handed her a glass, and she took it from him gratefully. The cold liquid cleansed her mouth from the acrid taste and soothed her scratchy throat. She gulped the cold liquid, feeling dry. When the glass was empty, she handed it back to Jesse.

"Thanks." Her voice sounded stronger. An incredible tiredness swept over her, leaving her drained. "I think I'd like to go home now."

The paramedic nodded at her. "It's probably the best thing for you. Stay warm and get into bed. Your throat is going to hurt for a few days, but you should be okay."

"Thanks," Valerie mouthed. Slowly she rose. Her legs shook like Mexican jumping beans on uppers. Matt put his arm around her, and she leaned on him, needing his support, wishing she didn't require his strength, but grateful for the comfort.

Fran rushed out of the restaurant. "I can't believe you stayed in there. The ceiling tile is charred. It could have fallen on you. You could have died."

"I just reacted. It wasn't until the fire extinguisher was empty and the flames were gone that I realized the danger," Valerie whispered and then started to shake once again as her mind pictured everything that could have gone wrong.

If they knew her past, everyone would think she had started the fire.

Fran shook her head. "I'm just grateful you kept the

whole place from going up in smoke."

"I didn't do anything anyone else wouldn't have done."

"You put out the fire. You overcame your fear and handled the situation," Fran said pointedly looking between her and Matt.

Valerie understood her message but felt too drained to react.

"Take her home and no fussing tonight," Fran demanded like an overprotective mother.

Matt frowned at her. "Fussing?"

If Valerie hadn't been so weak, she would have laughed, but she didn't have the strength. She managed to croak, "Someone take me to McKenzie's before I collapse."

Matt kept his arm around her as he walked her away from the fire engine and the crowd of people who had gathered in the street. It felt good to lean on him when she felt so vulnerable, so weak. He helped her into his Jeep and hurried to the other side.

He climbed in and started the engine.

Valerie was spent emotionally and physically. Matt kept glancing over at her during the short drive, and finally she closed her eyes and leaned her head back to limit their conversation.

"I owe you an apology for getting angry the other day," he said quietly. "I was wrong."

She groaned. She didn't have the strength to deal with the problems between them tonight. She whispered, "Please, Matt, do we have to discuss this now?"

"No, but I didn't take your suggestion very well, and I needed to say I'm sorry."

For a moment she sat stunned. He was saying he was sorry? How did she respond? She was too weak. At this moment, her defenses to his charm were completely obliterated.

"Apology accepted. Now can we continue this discussion another day, when I have the strength to complete it?"

"Deal," he said. "As long as you return to the office."

"Deal," she whispered. "As long as you take me home

Chapter Ten

The next day Matt glanced up as Jesse came through the door of his office juggling two cups of coffee.

"Hi," he said. "Since Fran's is closed, I thought I'd bring the coffee to you today."

"It's not that crap you make in your office is it?" Matt asked.

"Excuse me? The strength of the caffeine in my coffee has been known to scar many esophagi. Only real men are not afraid to drink my brew."

He sat the cups down on Matt's desk.

"Should I puff out my chest and beat on it?"

Jesse grinned. "Okay, I bought the coffee at the convenience store."

"Thank God for that." Matt leaned back in his chair.

The Sheriff sank into the chair across from Matt. "I thought about getting you one of those cappuccino's but knew it would ruin my reputation, buying sissy coffee drinks."

"You have such a macho lawman persona."

"Hey, watch it. I resemble that remark."

The two men each sipped their coffee. "Not as good as Fran's," Matt said.

Jesse nodded. "Speaking of Fran's, what did you think of that fire last night?"

Matt contemplated his response. "I don't know. The fire department didn't seem to think it was anything more than a grease fire."

"I know. But Fran has never gone off and left a burner on before. She's pretty careful in that kitchen."

"Yeah, that bothered me too."

Jesse gave Matt a stern look. "Okay, I'm here to confess."

"What?" Matt asked confused.

"I know I gave you a hard time about being suspicious of Valerie."

"Yeah, you did."

"I'm beginning to think that maybe I should do a little more checking on our girl."

Matt leaned forward in his chair and frowned at his friend, anxiety trickling down his spine like a babbling brook. "You told me you verified her."

Jesse nodded. "I ran her name through the database. A lot of Valerie Brown's came up. Not one fit the description of our girl."

"So what else can you do?"

Jesse smiled a devious look. "Well, last night when she asked for a glass of water, I kept the glass. I dusted it and lifted her fingerprints. We should know everything about her in just a few days."

Matt squirmed uncomfortably in his chair and leaned back while he contemplated this turn of events. Guilt and curiosity and fear consumed him. Did he really want to know the truth this way? "I don't think she's a criminal."

"We'll see." Jesse nodded his head.

"I've said all along that there is something different about her." Matt ran his hand through his hair, tugging at the ends.

"Or we both could be wrong about her. But after the fire, I think I should do some checking."

"You don't think she started that fire, do you?" Matt asked, feeling strange.

"She was alone in the café." He paused. "I don't know. It can't hurt to check."

If she was hiding something, Matt suddenly wanted her to tell him her secrets. He didn't want to learn the truth from Jesse. Yet there was McKenzie and the children to consider, and his curiosity insisted upon being satisfied.

"I think she's going to come back clean," he said,

hoping he was right. "But do me a favor. If you find something on her, don't tell anyone. Bring the information to me."

"As long as she's clean, that's not a problem," Jesse said. "After Fran's fire, I need to know if I have reason to be concerned."

Matt nodded. "I understand."

~

Two days later, Valerie felt rested. Her throat wasn't quite as sore, and she needed to see Matt.

He'd apologized, and that act of contrition had thrown her. She had never heard her father say the words "I'm sorry." Carter had never expressed regret for anything during their time together.

Those two little words had resonated in her mind over and over the last few days. He'd said he was sorry, and she thought she'd been hallucinating. A man never showed remorse for having an attitude about sex.

She had to see Matt. To be honest about why she'd taunted him, telling him she only wanted sex. Part of her had wanted to experience a night in his arms, while the other part knew she didn't do hookups.

She'd passed the restaurant on the way over and had seen the closed sign on the door. A truck was parked in front that had a sign on the vehicle, "Rudy's Painting." Obviously the remodeling to the kitchen was under way.

Valerie pulled McKenzie's Land Rover to a halt in front of Matt's law office. For a moment she sat staring at the building.

How much should she tell him? Everything? But if she confessed, then she would have to explain to the entire town, and there was still the chance her father and Carter were looking for her.

She didn't like lying to Matt, but she wasn't ready to

face her father and Carter. She wanted to enjoy this peaceful time just a little longer before they wreaked havoc with her life again.

Plus Matt would hate her for lying to him. Suddenly it was important that he trusted her, believed her, wanted her. She didn't want Matt to hate her.

She jumped out of the SUV and strolled to the door. She walked in, her heart thumping in her chest. "Hello. Are you here?"

Matt appeared in the doorway to the back area of the house, a spatula in his hand. "Hi."

"Hi." Her voice quivered at the sight of him. Dressed in jeans and a sweater, he looked good enough that she wanted to forget the take-it-slow part and just jump him. Do the nasty right there on the floor.

"Are you busy?" she asked.

"No. I'm fixing lunch. Have you eaten?"

Her stomach rumbled, reminding her in her haste to see him, she'd forgotten lunch. "No, what are you having?"

"Grilled cheese sandwiches."

"Sounds good."

"Come on back," he said, heading to the kitchen.

He flipped the sandwich on the grill and began to make her one. "How are you feeling?"

"Better. My throat is a little scratchy, but I'm okay."

Matt's green eyes searched hers, leaving her feeling flushed. "Fran told me you put the fire out."

"I emptied the fire extinguisher on the fire, is all."

"You like to live on the edge, don't you?" He shook his head. "You could have gotten hurt."

"I just reacted," she admitted.

"And you're okay?" he asked, his eyes searching her face. His hand reached out to touch her shoulder lightly, and warmth spread through her like a forest fire.

"I'm fine." She nodded. "Can you put some pickles on

there?"

He nodded and put her sandwich on to grill. "Dill?" She smiled. "Yes, dill."

"Me too."

Matt opened the refrigerator and pulled out a jar of kosher pickles. "Fix yourself something to drink and we're ready to eat."

"Okay," she opened the cupboard to grab a glass and their derriere's bumped. She glanced at him, and their gazes met and held for a moment. A tingle traveled along her spine, and she quickly turned to the faucet for cold water. It felt strangely familiar to work in the kitchen together side by side.

A pang of longing grabbed her midsection, and she realized she'd missed him. First their awful disagreement and then the fire. This moment felt right.

With one last flip of the sandwich in the air, he removed their grilled cheese from the grill and placed them on plates. They sat down at the table and munched on the cheese and bread.

When they finished their meal, they sat back and gazed at one another across the table, awkwardness in the air. Somehow she had to begin the conversation that had brought her over here, but she didn't know where to begin.

"You know you surprised me the other night when you apologized for your anger."

He raised his brows. "Why?"

"It's just that most men would never say they were sorry."

"Well, looking back on the situation, I was wrong," he confessed.

The fact he admitted he was wrong made her like him even more. She smiled and then became serious. "I realize that you and everyone else in town are curious about me. I've been a little secretive about my past, but I have a good reason."

He didn't move, but stared at her intently, waiting for her to explain.

"I also know that I didn't intend to come to Colorado and become involved with a man." She took a deep breath. "I came here to escape a bad relationship."

Silently Matt watched her.

"It's not that I don't think that the attraction between us is interesting. It's just that I am not ready to be in a relationship with any man. I've been here six weeks, and while coming to Colorado was the best thing I've ever done for myself, I'm not ready to be with someone else."

Matt ran his hand through his hair. "I don't want to be your rebound guy. But there is some kind of spark between us that I don't remember experiencing in a long time. I know you feel it too."

"But you're looking for someone to share that big house with, and I need time to heal from the wrong man."

Matt dropped his arm onto the table, making the dishes bounce along with her heart. Was he angry? "You make it sound like I'm going to install the first woman who comes along into my home like a dishwasher. Not hardly."

He lifted his glass of ice tea and took a sip. "I'm in no hurry. I'd just like to have fun together for a while."

She nodded. He made it sound so casual, yet it didn't feel that way.

"I'm willing to wait. And if you decide that we can be something more, I'm there. You let me know when you're ready."

"Matt, I don't want to hurt you," she responded. Why did she feel he only heard what he wanted to hear? Why did it seem that he wasn't going to give up?

Until she told him who she really was—that would certainly slam on the brakes. So why didn't she tell him?

"Who said anything about getting hurt?"

"I don't know how long I'm going to be here."

"None of us do," he responded. "In the meantime, we'll spend lots of time getting to know one another."

"Oh yeah?" she said. Despite her reservations, a feeling of warmth gathered beneath her heart.

"Most definitely," he responded.

That's why she didn't tell him. Because no matter what she thought or said, she liked Matt and wanted to see where they were headed just as much as he did. And the realization that her defenses were beginning to crumble frightened her. Especially since he'd made it very clear how he felt about lies.

And her whole existence here was a lie.

~

A week passed, and things were beginning to return to normal. The café had reopened with the kitchen receiving a new paint job and a new state-of-the-art Ansulex system. Valerie returned to working at the café morning through lunch, and then she worked for Matt.

And he spent every day anxiously awaiting the results from Jesse. It normally didn't take long, but this wasn't a criminal situation, and the lab in Denver was doing them a favor. So the results would come in their time, not Matt's or Jesse's time.

In the meantime, he worked on a new liability case that would take him to Dallas for a few days.

The door opened, and Valerie blew in with the cold breeze, bringing the aroma of spring flowers into the office, the smell of her perfume, soft and inviting.

"Hi," she said, pulling off her hat and gloves. "It's blustery out there today."

"Yeah, hasn't warmed up much." He watched as she bent over and shook her blonde hair, the curls tumbling into a gorgeous disarray that spiked his pulse rate up twenty points.

"How were McKenzie and the kids this morning?"

"The twins were still asleep, but McKenzie was good. She fixes me coffee every morning." Valerie hung her coat on the coat rack. "So what's up? Where should I start?"

Oh, how he wanted to answer that question with where his mind went. But he took a deep breath and glanced over at the stacks of paper on his desk. Each case represented a client in different stages.

"You can open the mail and see what's come in. I need a deposition for the Murdoch case and a lease agreement for Mrs. Carter typed. Other than that, it's been quiet."

"Good." She picked up the stack of mail and began to sort through it.

"Your voice sounds better."

"Yeah, I think I'm over the smoke inhalation."

He watched her as she bent over to pick up an envelope she'd dropped. Her jeans molded to her body, and her shirt rode up just enough to see a glimpse of the smooth white expanse of her back.

Her tempting display of flesh made him want to kiss each vertebra on his way down. He bit back a groan as he felt himself harden.

She bounced into the back of the house, her energy and vitality draining the room. He could pick her up and carry her into his bedroom, lay her down on his bed, and strip the clothes from her body. There he could begin to taste every inch of her.

He swiveled in his chair and tried to refocus on his paperwork. The pace of this relationship could be the death of him.

She all but skipped back into the room. "Hey, where is Mrs. Carter's file? It will take me about five minutes to type up her lease." She leaned over his desk. Her blouse dipped, exposing her cleavage. Her full breasts, round and shapely, enticed him.

His hands ached with the need to touch them.

She lifted the folders from his desk and glanced at him, her blue eyes filled with concern.

"What's wrong?"

Oh God, he could never tell her that the scent of her, the way she bounced through his office, her voice, everything about her turned his insides to mush.

"I need to get out of here for a while," he said, realizing it was true. "Let's go bowling."

"Bowling? But what about Mrs. Carter's lease? The deposition?"

"They can wait. I have cabin fever really bad and need to throw a couple of balls at anything. Come on."

He grabbed her hand and pulled her to the door, shoving her coat and scarf at her.

It took them less than five minutes to drive to the old-fashioned bowling alley. He parked the car, and the two of them all but ran into the building to escape the cold.

Tension for Valerie filled him to the brim, and he needed to release this energy without doing the very thing he wanted. Make love to her until her eyes turned green. And since they were blue, that was going to take a long time.

In the small town of Springtown, the bowling alley was the main hub of entertainment. The place was empty at this time of day, waiting for the night, when leagues would occupy the twelve old-fashioned lanes.

While she put her shoes on, he set up the machine. When he lived in Denver, he'd never bowled. But here, he bowled whenever he needed a diversion, and the bowling alley had become his place of escapism during the winter months.

Valerie's eyes shined bright in the dim lights of the alley as she gazed at him, keeping him at a slow burn. "I can't believe we're doing this in the middle of the day."

Oh, this was just a distraction from what he really wanted to do with her in the middle of the day. There was another form of exercise he'd much rather they were doing, but he'd promised patience. To wait for her, even if it killed him. He could be dead soon.

"You're up first," he said.

She stepped to the line, bent over, and he couldn't help but watch her cute little fanny as she threw the ball. She received a seven and ten split, but she didn't let that stop her. On the next ball, she threw across the lane, hitting the seven pin, sending it ricocheting into the ten pin. Stunned, he realized she'd just picked up one of the hardest splits in bowling. Beginners luck!

"Very impressive," he said as he took her place at the line. He hurled the ball down the lane with enough force to frighten the pins down. Instead he received the four-seven and six-ten split, which he didn't pick up.

She smiled at him. "I'm ahead."

"Not for long," he contended. He was determined to win, and this game was just a warm-up for whenever they did have sex. And they were going to find themselves together in bed, very soon if he had any say.

"How about a friendly wager," he said, feeling cocky.

"Depends."

"If I win, I get to kiss you, in my time, the place I choose," he said, watching the pupils of her eyes dilate.

"And if I win, you buy me dinner," she responded with a cooling glance.

"Deal," he said, thinking how this one kiss could lead to a second and a third. He had to win.

She threw her next ball, a strike. "I thought you said you weren't that good."

"I never said anything," she said with a grin. "You assumed I wasn't any good. My average in college was

253."

He whistled. "Well, I'll be damned."

For the next hour they battled one another. Sometimes she was up and sometimes down.

At the end of the first game she threw a strike with her first ball.

Valerie grinned, that saucy smile that made him want to kiss her until her lips were swollen. "Two more. That's all I need to put you away for good."

Matt frowned. He would do whatever it took to win this game. "Not going to happen."

"Oh yeah?" she taunted and lined up to throw her second ball.

"Telephone call for Miss Valerie Brown," they announced over the loudspeaker just as she went to throw.

The ball missed the pocket, and she had three pins left standing on the side.

She hurried back to him, a worried expression on her face. "That must be McKenzie. Something's wrong."

Laughter erupted from him, and he felt a twinge of guilt for tricking her. But he wanted, no, he needed those promised kisses.

She glanced at him, her eyes wide with realization. "You tricked me. You had them page me on purpose."

"Hey, you still have one more shot."

"And it's going to be a good one too," she said and marched to the line. Her throw was perfect, acing her spare.

Matt would have to throw an absolute perfect ending to this game. He doubted that he could catch her, but he was going to try.

As he walked past her, she popped him with her hand towel on the butt. "You play dirty."

Matt smiled. "I play to win at everything."

He let his gaze linger on her lips so she would know that he meant to win the challenge and kiss her. He couldn't wait to have her in his arms, his mouth moving over hers. Her begging him to complete what that single kiss would start.

With that thought he strode to the line, determined to win his reward. He rolled his first ball with precision, a strike. Two more and he could claim his kiss. He threw the second ball just as hard, and the pins scattered. A second strike.

One more and he could claim his prize. He stood at the line, the ball in his hand, focusing on the pins at the end of the lane. He began his approach, and when he went to release the ball, he heard her.

"Oh dear, my bra came unhooked."

The ball slipped from his hands. It rolled down the lane, missing the pocket. With a clunk it hit the pins, taking out three before the ball spun into the gutter.

He lost.

"Oh my," she cooed. "I don't think that's enough to beat me. I think I've just won."

He turned, and she had such an impish expression on her face it was all he could do to keep from throwing her over his shoulder and carrying her out of the bowling alley, where he would proceed to claim his prize regardless of the score.

"What?" She laughed. "I play to win."

"I think maybe I need to help you with that bra problem." He moved toward her. "Please God, let it be a front hook."

She moved behind the console, but nothing was going to keep him from reaching her. He chased her until he was close enough to grasp her arm and pull her to him.

He stared down into her eyes and felt his world tilt. "I'm buying dinner, but I'm taking my prize."

She smiled at him, that cocky irresistible grin. "I'd be shocked if you didn't."

His lips barely brushed hers. He didn't dare let them linger for fear of taking her right there in the bowling alley. "That's just a quick sample of what is to come later, when we're alone."

Her eyes went all smoky, and she licked her lips. "The sample was good, but I'm still resisting dessert."

Chapter Eleven

Later that evening, Matt walked Valerie to the door of his sister's home.

"Are you coming in?" she asked him, her heart racing with anticipation, knowing full well that he was going to kiss her. Valerie's knees shook with nerves. How could she want something so bad yet be so afraid? It wasn't like this was their first kiss. Yet, this kiss felt like the first time.

Why was that, she wondered?

"No." He halted at the door. "It's late, and the kids are probably asleep."

She glanced at him and swallowed, feeling more nervous than a virgin.

He drew her into his arms, hunger reflecting from his eyes. "I can't remember the last time I had so much fun at the bowling alley."

"When was the last time you lost?" she teased. His arms around her were solid and dependable.

"Whether I lost or won is debatable," he reminded her.

"Spoken like an attorney."

"Since the outcome of our game is in question, I think it only fair that I claim my wager."

She smiled at him, feeling happy for the first time in months. "If that's your way of telling me you're going to kiss me, I wish you would just get on with it."

He laughed softly and leaned in closer to her lips. "Oh no, I intend to take my time. And leave you wanting more."

His words sent desire spiraling through her, leaving her taut and needy.

His mouth covered hers, and she swayed toward him, her hands clasped onto his shoulders as desire sapped her strength. Her legs wanted to buckle as she rocked closer to him, aching to feel him tight against her, wanting this kiss more than she'd ever wanted anything in her life.

She opened her mouth to him, hungering for more than just the touch of his tongue, wanting the intimate caress of his flesh. A yearning ignited deep in her soul as his kiss pressed deeper and harder while his hands cupped her bottom and brought her snug against him.

She reveled in the feel of him, hard and strong against her. And the longing she felt frightened her. Longing led to loving, and so far she'd not been successful in that area of her life.

She broke the kiss and pulled back, opening her eyes slowly. She needed to regain some sense of control. "I think I better go in."

His lips touched her forehead. "I don't want to let you go, but I better leave while I still can."

Reluctantly, she stepped out of his arms. "Thank you for such a fun day."

He smiled and nodded. "Yeah, I had a great time."

"I'll see you tomorrow."

He opened the door for her. "Good night."

"Good night," she said and closed the door behind her. Part of her wished he wouldn't leave, yet she knew that was improbable, impractical, and impossible. Where had her resistance gone?

Valerie watched through the window as he bounded down the stairs and across the yard to his Jeep. For a moment she stood there and marveled at how spending the day with Matt had left her feeling great.

Oh, there was still a small wall of resistance, but more and more chinks appeared in that wall each day. And that both thrilled and frightened her.

Every day they seemed to grow closer, and if she closed her eyes and pretended that she were really Valerie Brown, not Valerie Burrows. she could see them together.

Funny how she seldom thought of Carter. She didn't miss him. Often, she thought of her father and wished she could call him. But she wasn't ready to face Carter, and talking to her father could mean she had to deal with her ex-fiancé. Right now that would be disastrous.

Because soon she would have to tell Matt the truth, and until she did, she didn't want to see Carter or her father.

The taillights of Matt's Jeep disappeared, and she slowly strolled into the living area. McKenzie sat bent over two scrapbooks.

"Hi," she said, glancing up, her eyes red rimmed.

"Hi," Valerie replied, concerned as she looked at her friend, seeing the pain on her face. "What are you doing?"

McKenzie sighed. "I'm trying to create scrapbooks for my children about their father's life."

"Oh." Valerie sank into the rocking chair across from McKenzie.

"Putting this together has brought up so many memories of John."

"Why are you doing it now?" Why would McKenzie put herself through such misery?

"Because his memory is slipping away from me. I hoped this project would bring him back. But it's made me realize, even more, that he's gone forever." A tear rolled down her cheek. "It's important for the twins to see how much we loved one another."

McKenzie swiped a tear from her cheek. "I'm sorry. Seeing the pictures makes me miss him so much."

"It's okay," Valerie said. "Tell me about John. How did you know that he was the one?"

McKenzie dipped her head, her look distant. When she raised her gaze, there was such a sweet smile on her face, though her eyes remained sad. "I didn't, at first. For a long time we were good friends. I could tell him anything, and he understood me. Then, one night he kissed me, and our friendship took a new turn. Six months later, I knew we would marry." She swallowed and looked at Valerie, her emerald eyes shining with sweet memories. "I've never been closer to anyone."

Valerie thought about her own experience with Carter. Had they ever been close? Would she have confided her problems to him? She searched her heart, needing to know why she hadn't recognized the problems between them.

Actually, being with Carter had never been easy. The only thing they'd shared was his profession being the same as her dad's and her father's approval. Nothing else. So, why had she agreed to marry him?

Could she have been seeking her father's approval? Was that her reason for agreeing to marry Carter? Her father had introduced them. He'd pushed her towards him, and when she'd expressed doubts, he'd reassured her that Carter would take care of her. She'd wanted to make her father happy and in the process become unhappy.

More and more, it made sense. She'd known her father would be pleased when she agreed to marry Carter. To gain his love and acceptance, she'd almost sacrificed her own happiness.

McKenzie interrupted her troubling thoughts. "So you and Matt went out tonight?"

Valerie smiled, the taste of his kiss still on her lips. The sound of his name filled her with delicious warmth as she remembered the day. "We went bowling this afternoon. Then he had to buy dinner since I won."

"You beat my brother at bowling?" McKenzie asked, shocked.

"Yeah, by two pins."

"And he didn't get mad?"

Valerie laughed. "No."

McKenzie shook her head and snickered. "I would have loved to have seen that game."

"Why?"

"Matt is one of the most competitive individuals I

know."

"Well, he lost tonight." Valerie wanted to talk more about McKenzie and her husband. She felt the need to understand the differences between her relationship with Carter and McKenzie's bond with her husband, John.

Valerie refused to settle for a mediocre relationship ever again. She would never let anyone persuade her when deep down she knew something wasn't right.

Whomever she was with, she had to know that nothing and no one would come between them. She wanted a connection that could withstand whatever life threw at them, in good times and bad.

She wanted a partner. She wanted a lifetime of love with one man.

"So what made your relationship with John different from anyone else you'd dated?"

For a moment McKenzie stared out the window, thinking. Finally she turned and gazed at Valerie, a sincere expression on her face. "John put my needs first. Always, even when he was sick. With just a glance, I knew what he was thinking. I wanted to spend all my time with him and no one else. He was always in my thoughts. I soon realized I loved him, and then, one night he told me he loved me. After that, we were only apart the night before the wedding."

"And your brother didn't want you to marry him?"

McKenzie sighed. "Our parents divorced when we were kids, and Matt swore he would never marry. The divorce is something he refuses to talk about, but I know it left him scarred. After seeing me and John, I think he realized that with the right person, marriage could be a loving, lasting commitment."

Valerie shook her head. "That's the key phrase. With the right person."

"I can't imagine trying to find someone else right now.

I still love John and probably always will." McKenzie wiped away another tear that slipped down her cheek.

"I hope you're not alone all of your life."

"No, but I don't know if it's possible to have two great loves in one lifetime. And I'm not willing to settle for second best."

With clarity, Valerie completely understood. "I know what you're saying. I came close to making a big mistake."

"You were married?"

"No, I was engaged. He's the reason I came to Colorado."

Valerie didn't say anything else. She didn't want to talk about Carter. She didn't want any sympathy as to what he had done. She wanted to put the past behind her and start her life afresh. She wanted to explore this attraction with Matt.

She enjoyed being with him. She thought of him often. They had a great time, and there was a rightness, a comforting presence when they were together. One look at him and she felt her blood give a little rush, and when he kissed her, she almost melted.

The fire, his apology, his offer to get to know one another had made her realize she should explore this thing between them. Yet, she was possibly wanted in Texas. Her father and Carter were probably still looking for her, and she'd lied to Matt.

How could she tell Matt the truth without him hating her?

She'd found so much more than she'd ever expected in coming to Colorado. She loved the life she'd created here, but how would Matt react when she told him the truth, and how could she stay when she'd lied about everything?

~

Valerie strode into Matt's office the day after the

bowling tournament. All night she'd looked forward to, yet dreaded, seeing him. Somehow she had to tell him the truth before they went any further.

"Hey," she called out as she took off her coat and gloves.

Matt sat at his desk, his briefcase open and a telephone in his hand.

"Yes, I need two tickets to Dallas, Texas, leaving from Denver tomorrow," Matt said into the phone. "Do you have an earlier flight?"

He stared at her, his eyes seeming to assess and fill her with warmth the cold outside couldn't touch.

"Okay, just a moment." He covered the phone with his hand.

"Can you leave tonight? We could spend the night in Denver and then catch a seven a.m. flight to Dallas tomorrow morning."

"What?" she asked, horrified. Panic surged through her, leaving her shaky. She couldn't go back to Dallas. She couldn't get on an airplane. She couldn't spend the night with Matt.

"I told you I have a case in Dallas, and I'd like for you to go with me," he said calmly. "I'm purchasing our airline tickets."

"I can't leave. I can't go with you to Dallas."

He frowned at her and uncovered the phone. "I'm going to have to call you back. If I give you a credit card, could you hold those tickets for me?"

"I'm not going," she said again for emphasis as he gave the woman on the phone his credit card information. Of all the arrogant moves, he was reserving the flights even though she'd told him no.

He hung up the phone.

"I told you no."

"Why can't you go to Dallas with me? The trial starts

day after tomorrow and should last about two days. I could use your help."

"For what? Why do you need me to go?" she asked, frustrated by his presumptuous attitude.

"I thought you could do some research at the courthouse on another case for me. We could have some fun while we were there," he said, his voice rising.

Of all the places in Dallas she didn't need to be, the Dallas County courthouse ranked at the top. As an attorney, her father spent a lot of time there. And Carter was there almost every day. Panic seized her at the thought of confronting her father and Carter. She wasn't ready. She liked the life she had created here. She wasn't ready for her life here to change.

"I'm not going." Anger crept into her voice. Last night she'd felt guilty for telling him lies about who she was, but today, once again, he'd pushed her.

"I don't have a driver's license. How could I get on the plane? It's just not possible for me to go."

"I'm sure Jesse could take care of your license for you. All we'd have to do is get you a picture ID, and they would let you on."

"And soon we'd be in bed together," she said, trying to divert his attention away from the picture ID. No photo ID-no law enforcement.

He smiled, and that just made her angrier.

"Don't tell me it hadn't crossed your mind," she said, her voice rising. Angry tears formed behind her eyelids and threatened to spill.

"I didn't say anything."

Yesterday they'd had so much fun together, and she'd anticipated being with him today. Her guilt over the lies she'd told him had led her to consider telling him the truth. Now all she felt was pressure. Pressure she refused to accept.

There was no way she could tell him the truth. Not now. Her secrets were safe for another day.

"I'm not leaving Springtown with you. Not today, tomorrow, or any other day."

Something in the tone of her voice must have gotten through to him as suddenly his shoulders stiffened. His eyes darkened, and she knew she'd finally reached him.

"Fine," he took a deep breath and looked down at his open briefcase. "I've got to pack. I don't have any work for you today."

She reached for her coat and gloves hanging on the rack. She yanked them on. "Have a great trip."

She walked out, slamming the door behind her. Yeah, it was a childish gesture, but it gave her a small amount of pleasure. Damn him!

Why couldn't he accept things as they were? Why, when she'd begun to accept their attraction, had he pushed her too far?

Cold afternoon sunshine couldn't warm the tear that slipped down her cheek. This was not how she had hoped to spend the afternoon with Matt. This was not what she'd planned. Damn him. She had to continue to lie.

$\sim$

Two days later, Matt sat in his hotel room in Dallas. The trial was progressing smoothly, and his client was happy. His trip was successful, so why wasn't he ecstatic?

Matt longed to go home to Colorado. He wanted to go back to his small law practice. No. It wasn't his law practice that drew him home.

He missed Valerie something awful.

He hated the way they had parted, and he couldn't sleep at night for replaying that dreadful scene over and over in his head. Once again his impatience had gotten in the way. He should have handled things differently.

He assumed after the wonderful day they'd had that she would want to go away with him. He'd been wrong. Something held her back, and until they crossed that hurdle, he had to learn to quit pushing her.

Matt picked up the phone and dialed his sister's number, needing to speak to someone other than the four walls that surrounded him.

"Hi."

"Hi," she said, surprise in her voice. "Are you home?"

"No."

She paused. "How is it going?"

"Good. I should be home late Saturday night."

"Great," she replied.

There was a period of silence. "You don't normally call."

"Is Valerie there?" he asked, unable to stop himself.

"Yes, would you like to talk to her?"

"Yes," he said curtly, not knowing what he was going to say. Only that he had to repair the damage he'd done two days before.

"Hello," she said, her voice sounding uncertain.

"It's me," he replied.

"Yes?" she asked, not at all friendly.

Unable to stop himself, he launched in. "Look, I know I pushed you the other day, and I'm sorry. It's just that I like being with you, and I didn't want to come to Dallas alone. It wasn't about the fact that I wanted to sleep with you, though I admit that thought crossed my mind."

Silence. Despair ricocheted through him. He was an idiot. He shouldn't have called.

"I didn't want to be apart. I wanted you with me."

Okay, he'd laid everything on the line. At this point, she could cut him off at the knees and it couldn't hurt any worse.

"I'm sorry, Matt. I overreacted."

"No, it was my fault," he said quickly, stunned at her apology.

"No, I didn't explain myself like I should have. We need to talk, but I don't want to do it over the phone. When you get back, I'll give you the reasons for my behavior that will help you understand my reaction."

There was silence for about thirty seconds while he considered everything she could tell him. It didn't make him feel any better.

"I'm not ready to give up on us," he said. "So, please don't tell me that this talk is a Dear John speech you're going to give me, because if it is, I'm not coming home."

She chuckled, which eased the tension a little.

"I'm not ready to give up on us, either. I just need to be honest with you," she said, giving him a moment of fear.

"I hear that the honesty thing isn't all it's cracked up to be," he said, trying to make a joke.

For a moment she didn't say a word.

"When are you coming back?"

"The trial should wrap up tomorrow. I expect to be home late Saturday night. Could we get together on Sunday?"

"Sunday afternoon is the Grahams' golden wedding reception," she said. "I don't want to miss it. They've been so nice to me at the café."

"They're my clients, and we've both been invited. Why don't we go together to the reception? Afterwards, we can go out to dinner."

"Okay, I'll see you then."

Another long silence on the phone and he knew they'd said everything, but he didn't want to hang up.

"Sleep well," he said finally.

"You, too," she whispered softly. "Sweet dreams."

"Good-bye," he said and replaced the receiver.

He wanted to dance. He wanted to sing. Somehow they

had made some small measure of progress tonight, and he wasn't sure why, but it felt good. She wanted to talk. She admitted she didn't want to give up on them.

He smiled. She wanted to be honest with him. And that couldn't be all bad, could it?

But God, he hoped she hadn't lied to him. The image of his mother came to mind, and he shuddered. His father's lies had all but destroyed her.

Chapter Twelve

Matt knocked on his sister's back door, before he entered.

"Uncle Matt," Austin cried from the table where he sat with his sister.

"Hi kiddos, what are you doing?"

"Colors," Ashley said, holding up a page that looked like a drunken rainbow with all different colors scribbled on the page.

"So you made it back from Dallas," McKenzie said as she colored part of Austin's picture.

"Last night about midnight."

"And you won your case?"

"Yes, I had a very happy client. He was awarded two million dollars."

"Oh my God!" she exclaimed, looking up from the pink bunny she was coloring.

"That's what happens when you drive drunk and kill someone," he acknowledged. "Where's Valerie?"

"She's getting ready."

About that time, Valerie descended the stairs in a short filmy dress that flowed about her like water in a gentle rain. The dress seemed more summery than winter, and he wanted to run through the sand with her while waves rippled around them.

"Wow," he said, stunned. "You look great."

She smiled, her lips full and inviting. "You look pretty good yourself."

Valerie glanced at the kids coloring at the table. "You guys aren't going?"

"No," McKenzie said. "I'm not chasing around toddlers with cake and punch in their hands."

"We would help you take care of them," Valerie offered.

"I know, but frankly, I don't think I'm up to an anniversary party."

Matt noticed that she didn't look Valerie in the eyes, and he suddenly realized that her and John's anniversary was this past week.

"You guys have a great time."

"You need for me to bring anything back?" Matt asked, wishing he'd remembered the anniversary earlier.

"Nope, we're good."

McKenzie jumped up and went into the cloakroom. She ran back and handed Valerie a lace shawl. "Here, you're going to need this with that dress."

"Thanks," Valerie said as she slipped the shawl around her shoulders.

"Let's go," Matt announced.

They waved good-bye and hurried out to the Jeep. On the ride over to the church they sat in awkward silence.

"Did you have a good trip?" Valerie finally asked.

"Yes, my client won," he said, glancing at her briefly while he drove. She looked like a model of sophistication and elegance and beauty that stole his breath away. Exactly what he wanted in his wife. And the last few days apart had seemed like forever.

"Congratulations. And the city of Dallas? How was it?"

"Warm. I had forgotten how much traffic there is." He'd been anxious those few days in Dallas, wanting to get home to Valerie. Needing to talk to her.

"Yes, the traffic never seems to let up," she replied automatically and then quickly glanced at him.

He frowned. She spoke like she knew the city of Dallas well. But she'd told him she came from Phoenix.

"So how long have you known the Grahams?" she asked, changing the subject.

"I met them when John was sick. Mrs. Graham would bring over food each day for McKenzie and the babies. She brought flowers and even stayed with the twins one day while McKenzie took a break."

"They're such a sweet couple."

"Yeah," he said as they pulled up in front of the church where the couple would renew their vows.

Valerie got out of the Jeep, her heels sinking down into the muddy ground. The snow melted during the day and then the moisture froze at night, leaving the ground soggy. She glanced at the Chapel and was reminded of the last time she'd been to church.

She pushed the thought out of her mind and on impulse took Matt's arm. He gazed at her, his emerald eyes warm, a smile on his lips, and heat sizzled through her. She'd missed him while he'd been gone. And though she dreaded telling him the truth, it was good to see him.

They walked inside the church, where family members were stationed at the door. "Welcome," one of the Grahams' grandchildren said. "Please sit wherever you like."

Matt and Valerie went halfway down the aisle of the chapel and took a seat.

"This is the first time we've been to church together."

She looked at him and smiled. "Yes."

Soft music from the organ began to play, and everyone hurried to take their seats. A few moments later, the couple walked down the aisle holding hands, followed by their three children. The Grahams' beamed at one another, smiled and waved to their family and friends that had gathered together to celebrate this special day.

Their love radiated from the happiness on their faces like a beacon, and with a sudden certainty Valerie realized she'd never loved Carter. She almost gasped aloud as the realization smacked her upside the head with clarity. This couple knew love, and nothing she'd experienced with Carter even remotely resembled the emotion they displayed.

If only she'd seen through Carter and known that he didn't love her, he loved the position in society that she gave him. And if only she had not accepted his proposal to make her father happy. Sadness consumed her with the comprehension that her own wedding had ended so badly, and the entire affair was a huge mistake.

Tears welled up in Valerie's eyes when she saw the love flowing from the Grahams' eyes. Carter had never looked at her that way. She'd never looked at Carter that way.

She glanced at Matt, and he smiled at her, his eyes a smaller reflection of what she saw in the older couple. And with stunning awareness she knew what he was thinking.

He was thinking they could be that couple if only she'd let this thing between them develop. If only she'd give him her love.

She almost choked and quickly looked away, back at the Grahams. They faced one another and spoke their vows, repeating each word with such meaning as their children stood at their side. In their seventies, they pledged their love to their last dying breaths.

Valerie peeked at Matt and tried to deny the feelings that enveloped her, frightened her. She felt so many things for Matt. Could these feelings be love?

Oh no, she couldn't have escaped a wedding only to come to a small town and fall in love with the first man who held her in his arms, making her feel safe. No, it couldn't be happening. It just couldn't.

Yet when she looked at him, her heart swelled with emotion. She wanted to only spend time with him. He was kind; he was fair; he apologized; he was a great man, and oh God, she loved him.

Fear threatened to overwhelm her and have her running from the church. It was too soon to care about him. It was too soon to fall in love. But her heart was bursting with emotion for Matt.

She swallowed, trying to keep the tears at bay. Tonight she intended to tell him the truth about who she was. But now…how could she when she loved him? But how could she not?

When the ceremony was over and the family had taken enough pictures to fill many albums, they urged everyone to follow the happy couple to the fellowship hall. There they greeted everyone.

When Mr. and Mrs. Graham saw Matt and Valerie, they smiled. "Here is our favorite lawyer and waitress. Did the two of you come together?"

Valerie hugged the older woman. "He picked me up from McKenzie's."

"Where is she?" Mrs. Graham asked.

"She stayed at home with the children," Matt replied.

"Give her our love," Mrs. Graham said.

They strolled away from the couple and were served a slice of cake and a cup of punch.

They took a seat at a table where she watched Matt staring at the couple's grandchildren, who served the cake, and their great-grandchildren, who ran through the hall chasing one another. "Wow, can you imagine that from the two of them most of these people came into the world. Can you imagine their Christmas? Their Easters and birthdays?"

"No," Valerie said, choking back the tears that threatened to spill.

Matt looked at her strangely. "I mean, you can see when they look at one another that they are still in love. I've never experienced that kind of love."

Valerie didn't say anything. She loved Matt and didn't know what to do.

"How about you?" Matt asked. "Were your parents in love, and do you have a bunch of brothers and sisters?"

She quickly took a bite of cake, trying to gain time while she cleared her throat of the unshed tears.

"I'm an only child," she managed to get out.

"Oh, I didn't know," Matt said. "What about your parents?"

"My mother died when I was very young."

Matt frowned and looked around the room again. "My own parents never could have created this because they hated each other so much. My father lied to my mother."

Pain reflected from his gaze, and she wanted to soothe him. She reached out and touched his arm. Could this be why he was so intolerant of anything other than the truth?

And now she'd lied to him. How could he understand when she'd lied about everything? Fear tied her insides into decorative macramé knots. What had she done?

"When I get married, I want to experience this kind of love. I want kids. I want the family table filled at Christmas and Thanksgiving with children and eventually grandchildren," he stopped and stared at her, a quizzical expression on his face. "I want a marriage that lasts forever."

A sob escaped from Valerie. A tear rolled down her cheek. How could she tell him the truth when she knew how much it would hurt him? Yet how could she not?

"I'm fine," she said automatically. She wiped the tear and drank from the punch.

"The hell you are," he replied. "Come on, we've paid our respects. We've seen the happy couple. It's time to go."

He didn't give her a chance to object. He took her plate and cup, strode over and put them in the trash. He hurried back and grabbed her by the hand.

"Let's go," he commanded.

They hurried out of the fellowship hall and straight to his car. It was a short and painfully silent drive to his house. He pulled into the garage and parked.

"What if we fixed dinner here tonight instead of going out? I think I have some steaks," he said, staring at her cautiously.

"That's fine," she said quietly.

They walked into the house, and when they were inside, he opened a bottle of chardonnay and poured them each a glass. He lit the fireplace to take the chill out of the room, and they sank down on the couch, their arms touching.

"What happened back there?" he asked. "Was I insensitive with my remarks about my dreams of a family?"

She gave him a painful smile. "No." She took a deep breath. "It's me, Matt. I watched the Grahams and I realized that the man I almost married, the man I ran from, I never loved. I almost married a man I didn't love."

"Why the tears? You should be happy you realized you were making a mistake and ended it when you did."

"It didn't happen that way." She took a deep breath. "I was dressed, and everyone was seated in the church. It was five minutes before I was to walk down the aisle when my best friend, Blair, told me she was pregnant by my fiancé."

Matt stared at her, suddenly understanding her reluctance to get into another relationship.

"What did you do?"

"I called Carter into the bride's room and asked him if it was true. He didn't deny sleeping with Blair. When I tried to tell my father the wedding was off, he took Carter's side. So I left. I ran out of the church and jumped in Carter's car."

For a moment Matt didn't say anything, and then he stroked her arm, feelings of tenderness overwhelming him. He wanted to go out and kick the ex-fiancé's butt for hurting her. He wanted to yell at her father. He wanted to cradle her, to protect her and promise her he would never hurt her if she gave her love to him.

The thought kind of startled him, and he pushed it aside.

"What does Carter do for a living," he asked, knowing instinctively he was a lawyer.

"He and my father are both lawyers," she said, confirming Matt's thoughts.

He laughed softly. "No wonder you know so much about the law and you don't want to get involved with another lawyer."

Valerie smiled at him, her eyes shining with unshed tears. "That's one of the reasons why I've been resisting this thing between us. I was afraid the attraction I felt toward you was just a rebound reaction. And I promised myself no more lawyers."

"Okay, I'll give up the law and become a farmer."

She shook her head. "And you'd be miserable."

"But I'm miserable when you're not with me," he admitted.

The smile on her face died away. "I missed you so much while you were gone."

"So you still think the feelings you have for me are rebound?"

She moved closer to him. "No, they're not rebound. With you things are different. I never felt such an intense need to be with Carter, like I do with you."

He looked into her sapphire eyes and felt himself harden. Oh God, he so wanted to explore the aching desire she ignited. But he'd promised her to take it slow. In the meantime, he was having a meltdown.

"Explain to me how you feel different," he asked, his hand running through her hair.

She paused. "Everything with you is different. It's more intense. Like it can't be denied." She took a deep breath. "And if you don't kiss me in the next sixty seconds I'm

          Sylvia McDaniel

going to die."

Matt groaned. "You don't have to ask twice."

Matt's lips came crashing down on Valerie's, and he loved the way she tasted of frosting and wine. She tasted sweet and tempting, and he wanted her with a fierceness that couldn't be denied. It seemed like he'd waited forever for her.

He wanted to taste her from head to toe. He wanted to forget dinner and feast on her for the rest of his life. His tongue swirled inside her mouth, teasing and tempting, his mouth mating with hers. Why did she feel like the person he'd been searching for all his life? Why did she make him think of home and hearth, children and laughter, security and comfort?

Valerie was the most alluring woman he'd ever met. Not in the way of looks, but rather more in her actions, her laughter, and the way she stood up to him.

His hands grasped her head while his mouth plundered hers. A moan escaped from her, and they fell backwards on the couch. He lay on top of her, his body full length against hers. He could feel her breasts, smashed against his chest, and she must feel him hard against her leg. He shifted until he was between the V of her legs, their clothes a barrier separating them.

She moaned deep in her throat, and he pushed himself against her, needing more. He felt like a kid in high school making out for the first time.

The phone rang, a clanging noise in the distance. Matt reached over, and with a flip of a switch turned it to silent mode.

He released her mouth and stared into her face. Her lips were swollen from his kisses, her eyes glazed with passion. Their breathing was labored, and he knew his senses were clouded with the smell and feel of her. She pulled his head down to hers and kissed him hard.

He groaned and knew he had to gain control or be lost.

Abruptly she broke off the kiss. She rolled out from under him, and he let her go with a sigh. God, he didn't want this to end. Not now, not like this.

She stood up, turned, and gazed at him, her eyes clouded with passion. In amazement he stared at her as she reached behind her and unzipped the back of her dress. Shocked, he watched as she slid the spaghetti straps down her shoulders and the dress dropped to the floor.

She stood before him in thong panties, no bra.

Without a word to him, she turned and walked toward his bedroom.

Chapter Thirteen

"Dear God," he exclaimed and almost fell off the couch in his hurry to catch up with her. His feet wouldn't move fast enough as he ran down the hall. He tore his shirt out of his pants and fought the buttons, finally yanking it over his head. Fumbling with his belt, he kicked off his shoes and shed his pants, almost tripping as he ran.

When he reached the bedroom, she had pulled back the coverlet of his big bed and lay curled on her side, waiting for him.

"What took you so long?" she asked, a smile of anticipation on her face.

She amazed him. She surprised him, and her beauty rocked his world.

"Oh hell," he muttered as he yanked his underwear and socks off.

He crawled naked into the bed beside her and took her into his arms. For a moment he just held her, enjoying the feel of her naked flesh against his. He gazed into the depths of her sapphire eyes and marveled at her beauty. God, she was stunning.

"I've waited so long to see you here, in my bed with me, both of us naked."

With her hand, she stroked his hair and brought his face close to hers. "Quit talking and kiss me."

She pressed her lips to his, and he returned her kiss, his mouth covering hers, his tongue stroking her with a passion denied until he felt like he would explode with anticipation.

Math problems. He needed to do math problems, to slow down the speeding climax headed toward his penis. *Two times two, is...* his hand stroked her soft skin. She was satin and silk to the touch, and he wanted to let his fingertips linger, but he yearned for more. His blood soared with the feel of her beneath his hand.

Oh, hell…he moaned. *Four times four is…*his hand reached out and touched her breast, and he pebbled her nipple with his fingers. She moaned, and the sound was hungry and wanting and needy, making him hard enough to burst.

Five times five would never get him through this night.

Reluctantly, he lifted his mouth from hers and placed his lips over her nipple. He sucked gently at first, lavishing her breast with his tongue, teasing her nipple until her breathing was harsh in his ears and her fingers clutched at the sheets.

He wanted this night to be perfect, he wanted to give her the greatest pleasure she had ever received. He wanted to erase her bad memories and replace them with slideshows that would arouse her every time she thought of him.

After weeks of persuasion, he finally had her right where he wanted her. In his bed. He'd gone from doubting who she was to only wanting her in his life, and he was determined to show her just how much he needed her.

His fingers slid over silky curls and delved into her moist center. He teased and plundered her intimately while she writhed beneath him. He kissed her neck, the sensitive spot behind her ear, his lips making their way back to her mouth. He wanted to hear her cry out his name. He needed to feel her tense around his fingers, and he wanted her pleasure before his own.

She grabbed his shoulders, her hands demanding as she pulled him to her and cried out his name as ripples of pleasure overtook her.

"Now," she demanded, and he smiled at her, only too happy to obey her command.

He opened the drawer to his nightstand and pulled out a condom. Quickly, he opened the foil packet and slipped the latex over his erection.

She lay before him, her chest rising and falling, her eyes smoky with passion, and he wanted to freeze-frame this moment, but couldn't. He had to have her now.

Matt layered his mouth over hers and kissed her until he felt they were one, and then he pushed deep inside her. She was tight and warm and slick with desire for him. And he knew that even though he wanted this night to stretch into forever, he wouldn't last long.

With each thrust of his body, she met him with an equal passion and fervor that had his blood soaring. Her arms wrapped around him, clinging to him as she moaned deep in her throat. She broke the kiss, and her eyes met and held his gaze as they reached toward that elusive crest.

The sapphire of her eyes darkened with passion and emotion, sending him riding the peak.

"Matt," she moaned.

He groaned, releasing the passion he'd held back, trying to hold out as long as possible. His mouth covered hers, almost eating her up as he reached his climax. He thrust into her, groaning into her mouth as he felt himself coming. She met his driving force and clung to him as she shivered with release. He reluctantly freed her lips, kissing her gently.

His heart pounded in his chest as the haze slowly cleared from his brain. Stunned at the magnitude of emotion overwhelming him, he swallowed and tried to regain his wits. How could sex one time with this woman totally blow his mind?

Matt sighed. Valerie had taken him to heights of pleasure, and though he liked to remain in control, she'd sapped his strength and wrung him out. He rolled them onto their sides, their breathing heavy, and their bodies glistening with sweat.

Yet he felt whole. Tonight felt right and special. So much more than just sex. Warmth, contentment, protectiveness, and an emotion he'd never felt before filled him as he held her. Could he be falling in love with her? He closed his eyes to savor the moment.

Slowly, he opened his eyes and stared into hers. They lay there staring at one another. She smiled and stroked his cheek. That simple gesture filled him to near bursting with emotion. But was it love?

"Wow!"

He shook his head at her. "Not a strong enough word. More like, *spectacular.*"

She giggled and snuggled closer to him, and he wanted to give her the world. "I think we should do it again, just to see if it's twice as good."

"Your wish is my command." He pulled her even closer.

Oh yeah, they needed to do this again. He'd known they would be good together, but could it get any better than this?

~

Valerie awoke the next morning with Matt's arm around her. They'd spent the night tormenting each other's bodies with pleasure, and now this morning she'd awoken with the shadows looming, frightening her.

Yesterday she realized this funny lawyer had captured her heart.

Matt was everything she could hope to find in a lover, a mate, a friend, and she had fun with him. They laughed when they were together. They teased one another. They talked about everything, and she'd shared things with him she'd never told her best friend. But she hadn't told him the one thing that could jeopardize everything.

She hadn't told him who she really was. And she feared he would hate her once he realized she'd lied to him.

Truth and trust were very important to Matt, and he would be angry that she hadn't believed in him enough to confess that she wasn't Valerie Brown.

At first he'd been so determined to see her on the next bus out of town that she could never have trusted him, and now…well she'd never intended to get involved with him. She was never going to get mixed up with any man, let alone another lawyer. And here she was in his bed.

She sat on the edge of the bed, unable to stay a moment longer. She had to get out of here. She had to get to the café. She had to slip away and call her father today.

Daddy could tell her how bad the situation was in Dallas. Then she would tell her father how she wanted to correct the past. Correct what she'd done to Carter.

When everything was corrected, then she would tell Matt the truth about her identity.

Matt stirred beside her, the sheet trailing down to reveal his strong, muscled shoulders. God, he was so handsome. He was a great lover. He was kind, he was fun and hopefully he was hers.

And she loved him.

She shook her head. She was so afraid. So afraid he would learn the truth before she could make things right.

So afraid he would hate her. By lying, she'd screwed up the best relationship she'd ever experienced. Funny, she'd never lied before, and this time she'd only lied to protect herself from her father and Carter.

Somehow, it had all backfired, and now she found herself in a precarious position. She looked around the room for her clothes and remembered they were in the living room. She tiptoed in, picked them up, and dressed before she headed out the door.

How was she going to tell Matt that she was not Valerie Brown, but Valerie Burrows, daughter of trial litigation lawyer Paul Burrows? A debutante. A millionaire. A possible arsonist.

Somehow, she had to convince him she'd had no choice but to lie to him. He had to understand that she would never lie again. Because she loved him.

~

Matt awoke to the sound of someone pounding on his door. He reached over and saw that the bed was empty. He glanced around the room and knew she was gone. The house sounded empty, except for the relentless pounding on the door.

"Just a minute," he yelled, reaching for his pants. They were still in the living room, where he'd yanked them off. He found some sweats and pulled them on before heading down the hall.

When he opened the door, he saw Jesse standing there with a smirk on his face. "Late night?"

Matt moved to let his friend come in. He looked around the living area. Her clothes were gone, but his left a trail to the bedroom.

Jesse looked at his shirt and pants, thrown recklessly on the floor, scattered down the hall. "Did I interrupt something?"

"Do you think I would have let you in if you had?"

Jesse frowned and held up a brown envelope. "I hope that whomever you were following down that hall was not our favorite waitress."

Matt felt a tremor of fear trickle down his spine. "You got the results."

For a moment he didn't want to know what Jesse had learned. Valerie had explained her secrecy, and Matt understood and accepted her explanation.

"Yep."

"It's okay. She told me she was running from a wedding, so it's no big deal."

Jesse shook his head. "It's quite a big deal. Our little bride is wanted back in Texas. Her father and her fiancé are on their way to Colorado."

Matt froze. "What?"

"I tried to reach you last night but couldn't get you by telephone, so I decided to come by this morning to warn you. Seems like I'm a little late."

"Wait. What is she wanted for?" Matt asked, his stomach tightening with dread.

"Remember that article in the paper about the bride running away at the church and then torching her fiancé's car?"

"Yes."

"That was Valerie. But her name is not Valerie Brown. It's Diane Valerie Burrows. As in Paul Burrows, the famous Dallas litigation lawyer. A Dallas debutante worth millions."

The blood drained from Matt's face. His insides turned cold, and he shivered.

She had lied. His mother's pained expression came into view, dredging up raw memories of his parents' divorce. He pushed the vision away.

Valerie had lied about her identity. She wasn't just no one. She was a debutante worth millions.

Everything seemed to fall into place, all his doubts about her confirmed. No wonder she was used to the finer things in life. She had come from money. But more than anything, she was hiding something and was wanted by the police.

Last night she'd had the opportunity to tell him the truth, but instead she'd continued her charade. And in the meantime, he'd given her his heart.

He sank down onto a nearby chair. "What's she charged with?"

"Nothing yet. But he could file criminal mischief. He's

threatening to press charges, and the insurance company is not too happy either."

Matt rubbed his hand through his hair. Why hadn't she told him last night? She'd told him about the wedding disaster, but she hadn't trusted him enough to tell him what she'd done or who she really was.

She wasn't a broke waitress, but a rich debutante. And she was Paul Burrows' daughter. *The* Paul Burrows, the most successful litigation attorney in Texas. The very man he'd modeled his own practice after. No wonder she wouldn't travel to Texas with him.

The thought of her deception pissed him off in a major way. How could they have any kind of lasting relationship if it was built on nothing but lies? Without trust, how could they have any kind of future?

"Damn!"

"Please tell me you're not in deep enough you can't get out."

Matt stared at his friend. "What the hell do you think? She spent the night with me and—Oh hell."

He put his head in his hands and then rubbed his face, trying to erase the painful heartache. Just when he'd thought they had a chance, he learned the awful truth.

Just like his mother, he'd been betrayed.

Jesse watched him quietly, not saying a word.

"I know I'm crazy for getting involved with her."

"I didn't say a word," Jesse said, throwing up his hands.

"You didn't have to. I should have listened to my instincts. I knew something wasn't right." Silence stretched between the two men, uncomfortable and strained.

"So what are you going to do?" Matt asked, unable to think of her in jail.

"I'm going to wait until her father and fiancé get here, and then, if the fiancé wants to press charges, I'm going to arrest her." Jesse folded his arms across his chest in his best warrior stance.

Matt cursed.

"What do you want me to do?"

"I don't know. It's just…the fiancé was a bastard to her." Though that didn't excuse her behavior. Even though she'd lied, he still felt the urge to protect her.

Jesse stared at him. "You're hopeless."

"What?"

"You're mad as hell at her, but you don't want me to arrest her," Jesse said, looking at him like he'd lost his mind.

Maybe he had. He'd dropped his guard, let her into his heart, and she'd betrayed him. She'd lied about everything.

It was time to set things right.

"I want her father to take her back to Texas. I want her out of my sister's house. I want her out of town." The hurt and anger were talking, but he couldn't shut them up. "And I'm going to go tell her right now."

~

Valerie looked up from wiping off a table and saw Matt and Jesse come into the restaurant. She smiled, and her heart puddled in her chest.

God, he was handsome, and her breath quickened. She loved him so much and was so afraid of telling him the truth. Would he forgive her for her deception?

He didn't return her smile, and then she noticed for the first time that Jesse and Matt were frowning. Normally, they came in joking with one another. Matt's expression looked like he was ready to tackle anything or anyone who got in his way.

Something was wrong. Her stomach tightened in fear. Could it be McKenzie and the kids? Was he angry she'd snuck out to let him sleep this morning?

Matt walked over to Fran and whispered something to her. She pointed to where Valerie stood filling a customer's coffee cup. He strode toward her, a determination in his step that didn't bode well.

"What's wrong?" she asked when he stopped in front of her.

"Outside," he commanded.

She set the coffee pot down on a nearby table and walked toward the door, her heart pounding in her chest. He was furious. There could only be one thing that would make him this angry.

As soon as they were outside in the cold, bright, sunshine, she turned on him. "What's happened?"

"Tell me your name," he demanded.

She swallowed hard and squeezed her eyes shut, wishing that she had told him last night. "Valerie Burrows."

"And you're wanted in Texas, aren't you?"

Her eyes widened. "I didn't know."

"You torched your ex-fiancé's vintage Corvette!"

"It just sort of happened."

"A burning car doesn't just happen."

His attitude went all over her, like a dash of hot sauce on a sizzling egg. "You have no idea what it feels like when five minutes before your wedding you find out that your fiancé got your best friend pregnant. You go into shock. You feel hurt. You get angry. So you jump in his car and run. But his damn car stalls in downtown Dallas, so I ended it for him and the car. I struck a match and watched that sucker burn."

"You broke the law."

"Yeah, well, I don't see anyone arresting him for screwing around."

Matt glared at her. "The worst thing is you lied to me. You lied and pretended to be someone you weren't."

His words were like a bucket of cold water on her anger.

"You're right. I lied. But I had no choice. I needed time to clear my head and find out who I am. I'm sorry that I didn't turn out to be the girl you thought I was. I'm sorry I wasn't the perfect little princess you wanted me to be." She took a deep breath, watching his face for any sign of a good reaction from him. Nothing. "I'm a damn good woman who had to outrun her father and fiancé in order to find out who she really is."

"And that new person turned out to be a lie."

She took a deep breath and stared at him. "No, the person who got off the bus was a lie. This Valerie, the one standing here, is the real person. A good woman who wants the same things in life that you do, a family and loving home. But if you can't deal with her, then it's a good thing you found out the truth!"

She was tired of being run over by men, and if he couldn't take her for the woman she really was, then she needed to know before they went any further. Valerie stood in front of him, trembling, her chest heaving.

"You know I would have understood. I could have even accepted what you did, until last night. You had the opportunity to come clean last night. You could have told me the truth. I thought we had something, and today I find out it was all based on lies."

"When did you want me to tell you? In the middle of my first or second orgasm?"

He glared at her. "You could have told me when you were talking about the wedding."

"Yes, I could have, but I wanted to be with you, and I was afraid if I told you the truth, you would act like you're acting now. Plus I wanted to call my father today and tell him where I was, clear my name and then come to you a woman with nothing to hide any longer."

Matt held up his hand. "Now it's too late. I want you out of my sister's house. I want you out of town. We're finished."

He turned and walked away, leaving her standing in the street feeling like her heart had just been run over by a tractor-trailer. For a moment she swayed, letting the pain his words caused roll over her.

If only she'd confessed the night before. If only she'd told him the truth.

She glanced toward the restaurant windows to see Fran, Jesse, and the other patrons staring out the window at her. When she looked over at them, they hastily drew the curtains closed.

How could she go back in there and face them?

She looked down the street to see an ugly green Hummer coming towards her. Sitting behind the steering wheel was her father. But the worst thing was that in the passenger seat next to him sat none other than Carter.

"Oh God, not now!"

Chapter Fourteen

"Valerie!" her father called, stepping out of the Hummer. "I've been worried sick."

There was silence as she tried to assess her emotions. Seeing him brought a lump to her throat, but then Carter stepped out of the vehicle wearing his two-thousand-dollar suit, and she went cold.

"Dad," she said, her voice chilly and rising at the sight of Carter. Was he here to take her back to Dallas and charge her with arson?

Carter strode toward her, his face beaming. "Darling, we've been looking everywhere for you."

She felt her insides twist into a knot, and she resisted the urge to punch the jerk.

"Carter," she said, her voice colder than a north wind blowing off the Rockies.

"I feared you were dead," her father said, anger in his voice.

"I'm not," she responded as she pulled her shoulders back, suddenly needing this confrontation. "Why are you here? How did you find me?"

"The sheriff contacted the private investigator we had looking for you," her father answered.

"Honey," Carter said soothingly. "Everything is going to be okay. Blair lost the baby. Now there is nothing to stop us from being together."

Valerie recoiled, feeling like a large toad had just slimed her. She wanted to sucker punch the loser. "And you think that makes everything all right?"

She couldn't keep the amazement out of her voice. How stupid did he think she was? "I don't know how to make this any clearer to you, so listen up. We are never going to be man and wife or anything else. You can jump back into the lizard mobile and head back to Texas."

She turned her back on Carter and faced her father, anger spilling from her, "And if you don't approve, then you're out of my life, too."

Her father's eyes widened in shock, and he stared at Valerie as if he'd never seen her before.

"All I want is your happiness," her father replied.

"Honey," Carter drawled like he'd just come in from West Texas where the land was hot and the days were slow. "It was a mistake."

"Stop!" she commanded. "Your penis landing in Blair's vagina is not a mistake. Now climb back in that car before my fist damages your pretty boy face."

This time she could tell Carter was finally starting to get the message. His eyes widened as if she'd grown an extra head.

"I came all this way to tell you we could be together." Carter puffed up at the finality of her announcement, indignity in his stance. "You burned my car. My beautiful Corvette! If we're not getting married, then I expect you to replace my car, or I'm pressing charges."

Valerie strode to within inches of him. Sarcasm seemed to explode from within her. "You're an ass. You cheated on me. But, you're right. After I left the church, it stalled in downtown Dallas, and I did everyone a favor, I torched the car instead of you."

There was silence for a moment as the two men stared at her as if she were an alien.

For the first time in her life, she felt in control. Nothing Carter said or did could ever hurt her again. Like a prize-winning boxer, she was ready to deal the knockout punch. "I know several very good lawyers. I want a jury trial with as many women jurors as I can get. Of course, I will be counter-suing you to pay for the ruined dress, the caterer, the florist, the church, and every other little detail in the wedding that your infidelity ended. Oh, and don't forget the personal humiliation I experienced. I'm sure that will get me a couple of hundred thousand."

Stunned, Carter stared at her. "What's happened to you? You're different."

He was right. She was different. She was more self-confident, self-assured, and she didn't need her father to take care of her any longer. She could manage on her own.

"The mountain air cleared my head. I'm no longer blinded by you. I see life a lot differently now," she replied.

Her father stepped forward. "Get in the car, Carter. You won't be pressing charges against my daughter. I think she's made a very good argument. I'll contact every newspaper in the country to make a laughing stock out of you if you even mention pressing charges again."

The younger man strode back to the Hummer, his back rigid. He crawled back into the monstrous vehicle.

Her father waited patiently until Carter was in the SUV and turned nervously to face her. "I don't know what to say, except that I love you and sometimes I'm blind in my love and need to make sure that you have the best of everything."

She wanted to forgive him, but the memory of his betrayal still stung.

"Daddy, I tried to tell you, but you didn't want to hear that Carter was cheating. Then you brought him here today. That's not exactly how to get back on my good side."

Her father closed his eyes and pursed his lips before opening them again. "I brought Carter here because I wanted to give you the opportunity to tell him how you felt. To give you some kind of closure. I thought you might enjoy telling him off." He frowned. "I'm sorry, Valerie. Sometimes your old man is an idiot. I was stunned by his cheating. I couldn't believe he would want Blair over my very beautiful daughter. After you told me, I went searching for you to tell you he didn't deserve my little girl.

I didn't want you to marry him, but you had already left. I screwed up as a parent. I'm sorry."

The steel band around her heart snapped, and she fell into his arms. He wanted to give her closure. He was apologizing. He had uttered the words 'I'm sorry,' and she felt tears in her eyes. "Oh Daddy, Carter wasn't the best."

"I know that now. It's just that he came from a very prestigious family. I ignored his faults because I thought you loved him."

She smiled and hugged her father. "I thought if I married Carter, it would make you happy. I wanted you to love me, and then when I told you about his cheating, you seemed to want the wedding to go on."

"Valerie, I love you, and I want the best for you. I couldn't believe what I was hearing. This insensitive jerk was cheating on my beautiful daughter. Later, I realized I'd been an ass. I should have kicked him to the curb along with his snooty family the moment you told me."

She smiled at the image and squeezed her father tighter. "Oh God, Daddy, it's good to see you."

He released her and looked into her eyes. "Let's take you home."

She leaned back and thought of going home to her old room, her car, and her life. Was that what she really wanted? No, what she wanted was in this small town, across the street and down several blocks.

"I'll send you to that spa you love so much. You can take one of your girlfriends with you," he promised her.

But it didn't feel right. It wouldn't make her happy.

Valerie shook her head. "You've spoiled me something terrible, and I never realized how much until I came here." She shrugged her shoulders. "I like living here. I'm happy, though I would like to be able to get into my bank accounts again. Eventually, I'd like to come home and get my car."

"You want to stay here?" he asked in shock.

"Yes," she said, certain that she didn't want to return to Dallas.

"I'm surprised." He laughed. "When I saw you weren't taking money out of your trust fund, I feared the worst. If you want to live here, I'll understand. I'll miss you. Can we call each other again?"

She swiped a tear that she didn't realize was there. "Oh, yes. I've missed you so much."

"Me, too. Can I come back to see you soon?"

"Anytime, Daddy, anytime. Just don't bring Carter."

Her father hugged her to him again like he would never let her go. "Always remember, I love you, Valerie. You're my little girl, and I love you with all my heart. Next time I'll listen."

"Next time, I'll be more certain before I walk down the aisle," Valerie assured her father. She smiled as an image of Matt waiting for her in the front of the church flashed into her mind.

"Call me, sweetheart," he said and walked back to the big green Hummer.

"I will."

"I love you," he said and climbed in.

She waved good-bye, relieved that the ugliness from the past was taken care of. Now was there any hope for her and Matt?

~

Matt sat in front of his sister, brooding. In the last two weeks they had argued more than when they were children. She had, in no uncertain terms, told him she was not kicking Valerie out. She had taken Valerie's side, and that rankled him big-time.

He was only here to see his niece and nephew, except they were napping. So he sat with his sister, the two of them barely speaking.

"So, when are you going to forgive Valerie?" she asked.

"Who said anything about Valerie?"

"I did."

"I don't want to talk about her." What was the point? They would never agree, and it would only lead to another argument.

"Too bad. I do." She said in a voice he'd only heard her use with her children. "You've sulked around here long enough."

Matt glanced at his stubborn sister and could see in her eyes that same determinedness that sometimes got him in trouble. He didn't need this.

"So, you were right about her. She wasn't who she said she was," McKenzie told him, folding her children's clothes while she talked.

He didn't say anything, knowing it would be better to just let her speak her mind. Then he would leave. His heart was bruised enough without his sister using it for a punching bag.

"Haven't you noticed the change in her since she got off that bus? Those first few weeks she was more skittish than a mother with a newborn baby. But over the weeks, she relaxed. The shadows disappeared from beneath her eyes, and she began to trust us. So do you think, after everything she's been through, that she *wanted* to lie to you?"

Why did no one understand his side? Why did it seem like all the women were backing Valerie, and the men just gave him pitying looks. "She could have told me the truth before I found out."

"And then what?" McKenzie asked, her voice rising.

He sipped his coffee. Could he just hit the rewind button and repeat his usual spiel? "Then I could have helped her."

"How did you find out who she really was?"

This was a new question and one he really didn't want to explore with his sister. He glanced at her to see if there was any chance he could mislead her and encountered her steely-eyed stare. Nope, she was on this like a bear on honey.

"Jesse ran her fingerprints."

"Nice," she drew the word out to let him experience her displeasure. "While she was lying to you, you were going behind her back to find out her real identity." His sister raised her voice. "And you don't see a problem with *your* behavior?"

"After the fire in Fran's kitchen, Jesse ran her prints, and then he came to me with the information."

"Jesse decided to run the fingerprints on his own?" she asked. "With no encouragement from you?"

He sighed. If he didn't come clean, she would soon learn on her own. "Yes, he did it on his own."

"You hesitated. Why?"

He took a deep breath, feeling like he was nine instead of thirty-five. "Because he told me he was doing it, and I wanted to know the results."

"And you knew that was wrong, didn't you?" she said. "Did you ever ask Valerie why she lied?"

"I know why."

"So you lied and she lied. Seems to me you both have some explaining to do. Nothing is ever just one person's fault in a relationship."

"Lying about who she is seems a lot worse than me trying to protect my family by finding out who was staying with you and the children."

"Please! Don't kid yourself into thinking you were doing this for us. *You* wanted to check out her background."

This was why he didn't want to have this discussion

with his sister. He couldn't win. He knew he was wrong.

"You keep saying that you want a wife and family, but your actions don't fit with your words. You say one thing, and then you act the opposite way. Being married is more than just having someone to come home to. There are sacrifices, doing things for the other person, wanting the best for them, putting your own needs aside, and that's before the children come along."

He stared at her, listening, though he didn't want to, feeling like she'd reached down inside his gut and was twisting it in an iron grip.

"But most of all you have to forgive your partner and love her despite her faults. So, do the female population a favor. Until you learn forgiveness, don't get married. We don't need another divorce in the family."

Matt felt like he'd been bitch-slapped. And part of him knew that his sister spoke the truth, even if he didn't want to acknowledge that fact.

He pushed back the chair, needing to get out of there before he said something he regretted. Without a word, he walked out the door, letting it slam behind him.

~

A week passed, and Valerie made sure everyone in town knew her real name. She even did an interview for the local weekly paper, telling them the story of how she'd arrived on the bus, a brokenhearted bride wanted for torching her fiancé's car.

She kept hoping that Matt would come to the café, but he seemed to have disappeared. She no longer worked for him. He'd sent her a note saying her services were no longer required. She kept hoping that he would see she'd only done what she had to at the time to protect herself.

But obviously it didn't matter. Everyone else in town thought her situation was funny, had laughed and teased her about being the "Wanted" Bride. Everyone but Matt.

Even Jesse had held out the olive branch and apologized for sending off her prints and contacting her father.

But none of them mattered. The only person she cared about held onto his anger like a shield and refused to come see her.

"You still moping around here?" Fran asked her late one afternoon as the last of the lunch crowd lingered over their meals.

"I'm not moping."

"The hell you aren't."

Valerie stood up and faced Fran. "Well, what do you want me to do? I can't change the situation."

The older woman laughed and shook her head. "You don't give yourself any credit. You stepped off that bus a scared, spoilt little girl, and I've watched you change and grow into a confident young woman."

"I was hardly a little girl. Spoiled, accustomed to the best, and scared, yes, but I was doing my best to hide that fear."

"Well you suck at being an actress. You didn't fool anyone," Fran declared, her hands on her hips.

"Maybe not, but I was determined not to go back to my father."

"And you did make it on your own."

Valerie nodded. "Only because you helped me."

"Hmm, I gave you a job and found you a place to live, but the rest was up to you."

"True. And I'm going to miss coming here every day."

The older woman's forehead creased in a frown. "What are you talking about?"

"Well, if I decide to stay, I'm thinking about opening up my own boutique. A women's shop with a small tea room."

Fran's shoulders slumped. "A tea room? What for?"

"Atmosphere. It will provide the boutique a unique setting."

"So, you're going to stay here in town?"

Valerie pursed her lips, her head and her heart in conflict. "I don't know. I want to. I like it here, but I don't know how much more I can take of Matt not speaking to me. He won't even come out to see his sister if he knows I'm there."

"He's a stubborn one."

"It's been three weeks. I should have gone home with my father. I guess I should buy a bus ticket and go home."

"And do what?" Fran asked. "Go back to the life that made you miserable?"

"And this isn't? Knowing you love someone and he can't forgive you. That's miserable."

"Give it some time, Valerie. He's been hurt, too."

She sighed and leaned against the mop handle in her hands. "I know I lied. I know I hurt him because he didn't know who I was, but he has to realize that I didn't like keeping the truth from him. I felt like I had to. For that matter, I didn't like keeping the truth from you or McKenzie."

"I know. But Matt is an all-or-nothing kind of guy."

"He was the one all fired up about us getting to know one another. I tried to resist him. I really did. It was never done to hurt him. I lied to protect me."

There was silence. "Damn. I really screwed this up, didn't I, Fran?"

"It's a mess."

"I couldn't forgive Carter, and Matt can't forgive me. Somehow there's some irony in all this."

"So why didn't you stay and fight for Carter?"

Valerie felt a spark of almost anger as she stared at Fran. "I never loved Carter. Not really, not like Matt."

"You ran from the situation with Carter. Are you going to run away from Matt?"

Valerie sat there feeling stunned. When she felt her father wasn't listening to her, she'd run from marrying Carter, unable to face her friends and family. She'd run instead of staying and dealing with Carter's infidelity. And now she was tempted to run back to her father because she didn't want to feel the pain of Matt's rejection.

What would hurt the most? Leaving without facing him, never knowing if she could have saved the relationship or feeling like she did now?

She swallowed and stared at Fran. "I don't like being hurt, and it hurt when Carter betrayed me. Now, it hurts even worse because Matt can't forgive me."

She set the mop aside, suddenly feeling angry. "If he thinks that I'm going to give up on us and run just because he's mad, he's wrong." She yanked her apron off and tossed it at Fran. "We're going to talk if I have to tie him down. Excuse me, while I go show him that I'm not running from this relationship."

Chapter Fifteen

Valerie strode out the door of Fran's café and into the bright sunshine. Her pace was quick and determined, as she'd never been angrier in her life. She hadn't meant to fall in love with Matt. She'd been a lost soul when she arrived in town. Life dealt her a raw deal, and the mountain air had cleared her head and helped her discover what was important. She'd had no intention of staying, and instead she'd met this jerk, this wonderful man, and fallen in love.

And now after chasing her for the last two months, he wanted to throw it all away. And she was just as determined to save this relationship and find out if it was strong enough for a lifetime.

The few people she passed on the street smiled at her and waved, but today she didn't feel friendly. She was unwavering in her resolve to settle this thing with Matt once and for all.

When she reached his office, she pounded on his door and called out his name.

There was no answer, and some of the fire burning inside her cooled. She looked down the street, trying to determine where he could be. Jesse's office.

She took off, heading down Main Street toward the sheriff's office. And then she saw him. Matt had his head down, his hands in his pockets as he walked toward her. Slowly, he raised his head, and his gaze locked on hers. He frowned.

"Matt," she called, and he promptly crossed the street to avoid her.

She halted for just a moment, stunned by the coldness of his action.

"Oh, no, you don't," she muttered to herself.

Valerie crossed the street to the other side of Main.

"Matt," she called, trying to catch up to him. "I want to

talk to you."

He tucked his head inside his jacket against the cool breeze and promptly turned into the barbershop.

She chuckled. Bernie's barbershop was the biggest gossip mill in town, and Matt hated the place. If he thought going into that all-male atmosphere would deter her, he was so mistaken.

She pushed open the door, and he glanced up at her in surprise. "We are going to talk."

"No, we're not," he said and walked into the men's room.

Bernie's shears were suspended in his hand as he stared at Valerie. Two older gentlemen waiting gave her cocky smiles.

Oh, no, this wasn't over. Not yet.

"Hello, gentlemen."

She strode to the men's room and shoved the door open hard enough that it slammed against the wall. Matt stood across from the urinal and the stalls, at the bathroom sink, washing his hands.

He glanced up at her in surprise.

"Are you freaking crazy?" he shouted in shock.

"I'm done with you walking away from me. You're going to hear me out whether you want to or not," she said, her chest heaving with indignation, her hands curled into fists at her side.

"Well, make it quick."

A strand of her hair had fallen into her eyes, and she shoved it impatiently away. "That Sunday at the Grahams' reception, the reason I started crying was because I realized I loved you. I wanted to tell you the truth about who I was. It hurt me to keep the reality from you, but I also wanted to make sure that I was free to offer you my love. I wasn't sure whether or not I was in serious trouble back in Dallas."

She took a deep breath. "I was running when I reached this small town and had no intentions of ever falling in love. After all, I'd just experienced 'love' at what I thought was its ugliest. I had no intentions of getting involved with another man for a long time. But then I met you, and slowly you won me over, made me realize that I had never been in love until now."

He didn't say anything, and she could feel her heart fracturing like a windowpane.

"You're right. I shouldn't have lied about who I was, but if I hadn't lied, I wouldn't be here now. I would never have gotten to know you, fallen in love with you, or learned the truth about myself. In this short time, I've grown up, and now I'm not running anymore. I want to be with you. I'm ready to show you I could be a great partner if only you'll give me a chance."

She paused, hoping he would jump in here at any point and say something, anything that would let her know he understood. "But I need you to forgive me for lying and give me a second chance."

She stopped and waited for him to reply. Silence filled the small bathroom.

"Are you finished?" he asked, his voice curt.

At the sound of a toilet flushing, they both jumped and a voice called out. "Now *I* am."

She felt her heart sink. She glanced at Matt, and he was frowning toward the stall.

She had to get out of here. "Well, I'm finished. I'm not going to beg you to give us a second chance. If this is what you want, you've got it."

Valerie didn't wait for him to respond. She yanked open the door. The barbershop was so quiet a termite gnawing on wood could have been heard out front on the sidewalk. She realized the men in the shop had heard every word.

"Is there any part I should repeat? Or did that come through loud and clear?" Before they could answer, she hurried out the door.

It was over. Matt didn't care enough about their relationship to forgive her for lying. And she couldn't stay in town and see him every day knowing he hated her. There was no reason to stay in Springtown, other than the fact that she had grown to love this little town and its people. But staying here would mean her heart would never heal. And she refused to face Matt day after day without his love.

~

Matt stared at the bathroom door as it closed. She loved him. She wanted them to explore a future together. And she'd asked him to forgive her for lying to him.

His mind went back to when he was a teenager. He'd found his mother sitting on the bed crying. He asked her what was wrong, and at first she'd said nothing. Then finally she'd told him his father had lied to her. He hadn't been forced to take the job in Tulsa. He'd found someone new. And then he'd told her he didn't love her. He'd lied about everything.

The pain on his mother's face had been a constant reminder of how the lies hurt. How men and women kept secrets from one another. He'd promised he would always tell the truth to the woman he loved, no matter what. He would never accept anyone who lied to him.

Yet, watching Valerie, Matt realized regardless of what she'd done, he loved her. And he even understood her decision to lie, but his pride had been smarting for days, and now he was torn between keeping his promise to himself and losing the woman he loved.

The stall door opened slowly, and Bernie's teenage son, stepped out. He glanced at Matt. "Is it all clear? Can I come out?"

Matt smiled. "She's gone."

The boy shook his head. "Wow, she was really buggin'."

"Yeah," Matt said, not wanting to talk about Valerie.

"I mean, dude, she's totally nuts about you. And you can't blame her for lying. I mean, come on, she was one kick-ass bride to set her fiancé's car on fire!"

"How do you know so much about Valerie?" Matt asked the kid.

"Hey, we talked about her story in our Social Studies class. She was a current event. We all thought it was cool that she's been hiding in our town since January. I mean, talk about dumped at the last second. Can you imagine the embarrassment?"

Matt stared at the kid and tried to place himself in Valerie's position. Dressed, ready and waiting to walk down the aisle, and your best friend tells you she's pregnant by your man. He sighed. He guessed he'd have done more than set the guy's car on fire.

"Crap."

"Yeah, man, and now the two of you are splitting. You don't have a cool car, do you? They don't call her the "Wanted" Bride for nothing."

"Just an old Jeep."

"Too bad you guys are splitting. She's really cool." The kid leaned forward and whispered, "I don't think she meant to hurt you. She just didn't want anyone to know where she was."

What the hell! A fourteen-year-old was giving him advice. And Matt looked and felt like a jerk. Especially since he knew he was overreacting because of his own stuff. His parents' divorce still affected his thinking, his decisions, and it was time to stop. It was time to make his own choices, even his own mistakes. Though in his gut, it didn't feel like a mistake with Valerie.

"Hey, Bryan, do you think we can keep this conversation under wraps and not have it flying on the Internet?"

"Well…I can try, but I sent a text message to my friend while I was hiding in the stall."

Matt shook his head. "Then you owe me a favor."

"What?"

"Do a follow-up text message later tonight on the outcome."

"The outcome?"

"Yeah, I've got to go find her and hope she'll give me a chance to talk."

The kid grinned. "Deal."

~

Valerie went straight to McKenzie's and hurried up the stairs without speaking to anyone. She pulled her suitcases out of the closet and threw them on the bed, where she proceeded to empty the closet of what was left of her honeymoon wardrobe. So many useless clothes that were certainly not warm enough for Colorado.

The woman who wore all these clothes, she no longer existed. The old Valerie had been a spoilt kid who thought of only herself and the latest fashions. She was a different person now. A better person.

She had survived heartache before, and she would again, though this time the hurt was deeper.

A tear slipped down her cheek and then another. Soon they were rolling heedlessly down her face. She refused to stop packing, and occasionally she would wipe away the moisture.

McKenzie came to the doorway and watched her for a few moments. "So, you're leaving?"

Valerie glanced up at her and nodded. "It's over. I'm

going home."

McKenzie walked over and hugged her and then kissed the top of her head. "I'm sorry my brother is so stubborn and bullheaded. He's giving up the best."

Valerie leaned back and wiped her eyes. "Thanks. I'm going to miss you and the kids."

"Oh, honey, we'll miss you, too."

McKenzie stepped back to the door, and suddenly a child crying could be heard. "Oh, dear, that's the *"I'm hurt"* cry. I'll be right back."

Valerie picked up her second suitcase and started pulling clothes out of the drawers. She threw them haphazardly into the bag. She had to get out of town tonight, and the bus was due in an hour.

She hated leaving. Yet, she knew she must. She couldn't face seeing Matt each day, loving him from a distance.

She went into the closet and pulled out her Jimmy Choo shoes, the ones she'd worn when she arrived in town. They were impractical in the snow and slush, and she'd forgotten how much she liked them. She put them in the suitcase and promised herself that she would not return to Dallas and go back to being the spoiled princess she once was.

Valerie heard McKenzie in the doorway. She didn't look up. "That sounded like Austin, was he okay?"

"His sister smacked him for acting stupid, just like his uncle," Matt said, his voice low.

Valerie glanced up, startled, confused by his statement. "What are you doing here? Did McKenzie call you?"

"No, I came on my own."

She stared at him. "Why? What do you want?"

"You've had your chance to talk. Now it's mine."

For a moment she was shocked. What was left to say?

She stood taller, squared her shoulders, and met his gaze.

"I've been an ass. Since the time my father lied to my mother and left us, I made a pledge to myself that I would never lie to women and I would expect the same from anyone I was involved with. In these past weeks, I've struggled to come to terms with your lying to me about who you were. I knew you were confused, and I knew why you lied, but I kept coming back to that same commitment I'd made to myself not to accept anyone who lied."

He took a step toward her into the room. "I've had to come to terms with the fact that even though trust is important to me, understanding what's happening is even more important. I got confused. You're more important. I need you in my life with me. I want to see if the love we feel is enough for a lifetime." He paused for a moment as if searching for something to say. "Can we start from here?"

She felt confused. What was he saying?

"Can we start over?" he asked. He held out his hand. "Hi, I'm Matt, I'm the local attorney."

A sob escaped from her, and tears trailed down her face. She took his hand. "I'm Valerie Burrows."

He pulled her into his arms. "God, I've missed you so much."

"Me, too."

"Sometimes, I can be an idiot. Love me enough to help me through those times," he told her.

She loved the way his arms felt around her. "I don't think you're going to be able to run the "Wanted" Bride out of town."

"Good," he said and kissed her. "You belong here with me."

"Always," she whispered against his shirt. "Always."

Thank you for reading!

Dear Reader,

Thank you so much for reading *The Wanted Bride*. Whether you loved the book or hated it, I would appreciate it if you let everyone know by leaving a few words on your favorite vendor's website.

If you enjoy western historical authors, please join the Pioneer Hearts group on Facebook. This is a fabulous group of readers and authors who enjoy westerns.

Sign up for my newsletter at sylviamcdaniel.com if you'd like to learn about my new releases as soon as possible.

Reading one of my books is like spending time with me, and I just want to say thank you from the bottom of my heart.

Yours in Drama, Divas, Bad Boys, and Romance!
Sincerely,
Sylvia McDaniel

Books by Sylvia McDaniel

Contemporary Romance

Standalones
The Reluctant Santa
My Sister's Boyfriend
The Wanted Bride
The Relationship Coach
Her Christmas Lie
Secrets, Lies, and Online Dating
Paying for the Past
Cupid's Revenge

Anthologies
Kisses, Laughter & Love
Christmas with you

Collaborative Series

Magic, New Mexico
Touch of Decadence

Western Historicals

Standalones
A Hero's Heart
A Scarlet Bride
Second Chance Cowboy

The Cuvier Women
Wronged
Betrayed
Beguiled

Lipstick and Lead
Desperate
Deadly
Dangerous
Daring
Determined
Deceived

Scandalous Suffragettes
Abigail
Bella
Callie
Faith

The Burnett Brides
The Rancher Takes a Bride
The Outlaw Takes a Bride
The Marshal Takes a Bride
The Christmas Bride

Anthologies
Wild Western Women
Courting the West
Wild Western Women Ride Again

Collaborative Series

The Surprise Brides
Ethan

American Mail Order Brides
Katie

About the Author

Sylvia McDaniel is a best-selling, award-winning author of historical romance and contemporary romance novels. Known for her sweet, funny, family-oriented romances, Sylvia is the author of The Burnett Brides, a western historical western series, The Cuvier Widows, a Louisiana historical series, and several short contemporary romances.

She is the former President of the Dallas Area Romance Authors, a member of the Romance Writers of America®, and a member of Novelists Inc. Her novel, A Hero's Heart, was a 1996 Golden Heart Finalist. Several other books have placed or won in the San Antonio Romance Authors Contest and the LERA Contest, and she was a Golden Network Finalist.

Married for nearly twenty years to her best friend, they have two dachshunds that are beyond spoiled and a good-looking, grown son who thinks there's no place like home. She loves gardening, shopping, knitting, and football (Cowboys and Bronco's fan), but not necessarily in that order.

Look for her the first Tuesday of every month at the Plotting Princesses blogspot, and be sure to sign up for her newsletter to learn about new releases and contests. Every month a new subscriber is entered into a drawing for a free book!

She can be found online at: www.sylviamcdaniel.com or on Facebook. You can write to Sylvia at P.O. Box 2542, Coppell, TX 75019.

family has been killed, Sabrina's loved ones are in danger, and something is not right in Sherwood. Can he claim justice for his family and reclaim Sabrina's heart? Or will old hurts tear them apart before he has the chance to prove his commitment?

Sneak Peek into Second Chance Cowboy

1878

Shadows from the courthouse settled over Sabrina Callahan as she hurried down the street of Sherwood, bringing back the unpleasant memories of her brother's cattle rustling trial. The smell of justice—a mixture of fear, greed, and retribution—filled her nostrils. It was the reason she'd left town so long ago, a nagging ache now instead of the raging heartache she'd once experienced.

The telegram crackled in her reticule, reminding her of its message and the reason for her return. Whoever had sent the telegram had left his name off the unwelcome notice.

The same clapboard buildings lined Main Street, their fronts faded by the hot Texas sun. The closer she came to the sheriff s office, the louder and clearer the shouts of two angry voices smote her ears. Weary from her journey, she climbed the steps, her hand reaching for the door knob.

A deep, masculine voice resounded from the other side of the door. Somehow that voice was familiar...

"Dammit, Sheriff, neither the Comanche nor the Kickapoo would have burned out our ranch. My father was friendly with both of them."

"I know this is hard for you to believe, but them redskins, they ain't loyal to nobody. Hell, I was out there the next morning. Evidence clearly showed it was Indians."

"Sheriff, anybody could have made it appear it was Indians."

A cold sweat broke out on her skin. That deep timbre could only belong to one person: Patrick Shand.

The man who had arrested her brother. The reason she had left Sherwood. The man she had once loved and been engaged to.

The same older voice stated, "I've heard all the rumors. You're goin' around accusing Carson Jarvis because of that damned trial. I'm warning you; this is the last time I want to hear you blaming anyone but Indians." The shouting voice softened. "I'm sorry, son; it's been six months. I'm closing this case today. I've wasted enough time on it."

There was a silence that seemed to stretch into eternity. Finally, Patrick responded. "Go ahead. Close your damn investigation, but that doesn't mean I'll stop looking for their killers: And when I find them, it won't be Indians."

Patrick's ranch had burned? What else had happened in the two years since she'd been gone? Should she stay and face Patrick or run and hide? Two years was a long time, but was it long enough to bury the hurt that had driven them apart?

Boot heels smacked across the hard floor. Before Sabrina could react, the door was yanked open, jerking the knob from her hand. It was too late to run, too late to hide.

Frozen in the doorway, she stood face to face with the man she had hoped never to see again. The man who had broken her heart

Patrick Shand towered above her, anger radiating from him. Tall, handsome Patrick, with eyes the color of Texas sand, sparked with streaks of gold. As the shock of recognition faded, a grin curved his full lips.

Sabrina's heart hammered inside her ribs as she stepped back against the porch railing. His eyes raked her in a sweeping inspection. Cringing, she realized how dirty she must look after her long stagecoach ride. Dust coated her clothing and skin like a fine powdery mist, yet Patrick looked good, too good.

The years had changed him for the better. Her eyes unwillingly feasted on him, noting the places his body had filled out. A stubble of beard was beginning to show on his cheeks and the hard line of his jaw, enhancing his rugged good looks.

"Well, if it ain't my lucky day! Look whose back from her fancy boarding school." Patrick pushed his hat back from his face as though to make sure it was really Sabrina. "Do they teach eavesdropping or was this a talent I never knew about?"

Sabrina bristled. The years had not softened his sharp tongue. "Why would I want to eavesdrop on your conversation?" How could she ever have loved this arrogant man? She lifted her heavy skirts and swept past him, clearly dismissing him.

He moved aside and then called to her. "I'm wounded. You have nothing to say to your old fiancé? Rehash old times? Maybe even greet me with a welcoming kiss?"

Why didn't he go away? After a grueling week of worry, he was the last person she wanted to see.

Sabrina turned and leveled her best glare at him. It had always worked on her students at the academy, but Patrick was not easily intimidated, and the smile he returned was not only challenging, but beguiling with his full lips and twinkling eyes.

That smile and those eyes—in a previous life were characteristics she'd loved about him.

"If I remember correctly, we said everything there was to say in front of the whole town two years ago." Her voice sounded empty of emotion, though her heart pulsated in a nervous rhythm. She *was* over him, though her pulse raced with remembrance.

Clearly dismissing Patrick, she whirled around to confront the sheriff. But the face before her brought her to an immediate halt. "Where's Sheriff Earl?"

Patrick stepped up beside Sabrina. "Sabrina Callahan, meet our new sheriff, John Sims."

The law officer sat behind a battered desk, his feet propped up, and his arms crossed behind his head, relaxing against the wall. Obviously, this man enjoyed his food, as his stomach and chest seemed to blend together. She stared at a hole in the sole of his boot, his red sock shining through like a beacon.

"Nice to meet ya,' Miss Callahan. What can I do for you, ma'am?" He smiled a toothless grin and then proceeded to spit over his right shoulder. Spittle pinged inside the brass spittoon, sending a shudder through Sabrina.

"What happened to Sheriff Earl?" Sabrina asked as she watched the sheriff move the wad of tobacco from cheek to cheek.

"Got shot in the back one night."

Sabrina frowned. Sheriff Earl was dead. Her father's closest friend was gone, and no one had informed her. Things had changed in Sherwood, and judging from the telegram she had in her reticule, not all for the better.

"My father is Jed Callahan." Sabrina clutched the telegram tightly in her hand. "I received this telegram saying he had been shot." For three hundred miles, she had read and reread that small piece of paper, wondering how seriously injured her father was, wondering if she would make it home in time, praying she wasn't too late. Anxiously, she asked, "Is he all right?"

"Miss Callahan, your father's gonna be okay." The sheriff crossed his arms over his large stomach dismissively.

Sabrina frowned at the sheriff. "What happened?"

Sims scratched his head. "Jed don't remember too much from that day. We've been having trouble with rustlers around here. The way I figure it, he stumbled on them stealing cattle and tried to take them on by himself."

"Our distinguished sheriff hasn't caught many criminals since he took office," Patrick's cool voice stated.

"Shut up, Shand. I've had all I'm gonna take from you today," the sheriff shouted, wagging his finger.

"Do you have any suspects?" Sabrina pleaded, frustrated by the man's uncaring attitude.

"Now, Miss Callahan, don't you worry that pretty head of yours about this. We'll catch whoever shot your father."

Sabrina's blood began a slow boil. First Patrick's reappearance and now this overweight, spitting bore was speaking to her as if she had mush for brains.

"If rustlers were in the area, why weren't you out there looking for them? Where were you the day he got shot?" Sabrina watched the sheriffs face turn a satisfying shade of red.

The sheriff bristled. "Now, Miss Callahan, I got enough responsibilities right here in this town to keep me busy. You ranchers have more than enough hired help to protect you."

Patrick burst out laughing. "Tell the truth, Sims. You don't sit well astride a horse and you might miss a meal if you were out on the trail."

"Dammit, Shand! Get the hell out of my office or I'm going to throw you in jail."

"Whatever you say, Sims." Patrick put his hat on his head and started for the door. The clatter of his boots on floorboards echoed in the small room.

The sheriff said, "Miss Callahan, I'm a busy man. I have work to do." He was clearly dismissing her.

"I'll leave you to your work," Sabrina replied sarcastically, all pretense gone from her voice, "...after you tell me if you've seen any of the riders from the Big C today. I need a ride to the ranch."

She had no transportation. No one was expecting her, and until this moment she had expected Sheriff Earl to take her home.

The sheriff shuffled papers on his desk. "No. Can't say that I have. You might check with the doc though. He's been riding out to your ranch every day to check on your father."

Patrick paused, his hand on the door latch. "The doc just left to deliver a baby. I'm headed in your direction." His voice was cool, not at all inviting. She turned and regarded him with animosity. "No, thank you."

A mocking smile touched his lips as he raised his brows. "How do you plan on getting home?"

He knew she had no way home and he was using it to his advantage. Sabrina sighed. "I guess I don't have a choice."

"Not really," Patrick stated with a smirk on his face. He opened the door, obviously expecting cooperation from Sabrina. Part of her wanted to deny him, wait until tomorrow, but the thought of her father made her swallow her pride.

"Let's go." Sabrina replied.

"After you, my lady." His voice was heavy with sarcasm. Touching the rim of his hat, he glanced back at the sheriff. "Don't work too hard, Sims."

The sheriff spat again over his shoulder, missing the spittoon. A stream of tobacco juice slid down the wall. Sabrina hurried out the door.

Patrick loaded her trunk in the back of the wagon and they quickly headed out of town. Despite the awkwardness of the situation, Sabrina sat back and relished the feeling of being close to home.

The west Texas countryside shimmered in the warm spring sun and welcomed her home. The fresh scent of honeysuckle floated in the air, announcing spring's arrival.

Across the prairie, bluebonnets, orange Texas paints and yellow buttercups blended, splashing color against the green grass. Mesquite trees stood against the sky like gnarled old men.

Out of the corner of her eye, Sabrina gazed at the man sitting next to her. Strong, sturdy hands gripped the reins, controlling the horses. The memory of those hands holding her, kissing her, returned leaving her aching from long-ago memories. The muscles in his arms strained the fabric of his shirt. Over long, muscular thighs, his blue pants fit snugly. The innocence of youth was gone and left behind was a man, hard and dangerous.

A stray lock of sandy hair fell from beneath his hat and grazed his forehead. A sudden urge to reach over and brush it back with her fingertips assailed her, but wisely she kept her hands to herself.

Patrick turned to her with a curious expression. "I don't remember Jed saying you were coming home."

Sabrina sighed and pushed a strand of blonde hair beneath her bonnet. She should have known her father and Patrick would have kept in touch, even after the broken engagement.

"He doesn't know I'm coming."

"That's what I thought." Patrick stared ahead, avoiding her gaze. "Why did you come home?"

"I was worried about my father." And the ranch: The other line of the telegram had said the ranch was in financial trouble.

Warm wind struck her full in the face as he brought the wagon over the crest of a ridge. Anxiously, she asked, "Have you seen my father? How badly is he hurt?"

"He's fine. The doctor wanted him to stay in bed a couple more days, but Jed refused."

"What does Dad say about the shooting?"

"He rode up on them before he actually saw them. By the time he pulled his gun, it was too late. The bullet grazed his head, knocking him unconscious. Then they left him for dead."

Sabrina's hands gripped the wagon tighter. Her father could have been killed. And no one had felt she needed to know except the mysterious telegram writer. "Did you send me a telegram?"

Patrick gazed at her oddly. "Why would I send *you* a telegram?" A puzzled expression crossed his face. "I didn't even know where you were. Wasn't there a name on it?"

"No." Sabrina watched the wind whip across Patrick's face. "Maybe Matt forgot to sign it."

"Maybe."

"I certainly never expected to find you in Sherwood. Last I heard, you were never coming back." She adjusted her bonnet as the wind tried to whip it from her head.

Patrick's face turned grim. "I came home to find my family's killers."

Sabrina gasped. "Your family was murdered!"

It seemed as if Dad's letters had been trivial. Filled with nothing, telling her nothing, leaving her in the dark regarding what really was going on in Sherwood. Quietly, she said, "I didn't know. What happened?"

"Someone attacked the ranch and killed Mom and Dad. When I came home, the house was burned to the ground and the stock were all scattered to hell and gone. The sheriff says it was Indians, but I don't believe him." His voice sounded empty.

Horrified, Sabrina replied, "I'm so sorry."

She reached out to touch his arm in a comforting gesture, but he pulled away from her touch. She saw his clenched jaw, the rigid manner in which he held the reins. Patrick had always been a proud man, much too arrogant to let her comfort him, but maybe it was better this way.

Touching him would only bring back pleasant memories which didn't need to be revived.

"Your parents were always kind to me." Patricia Sand had consoled her those painful days after Patrick left Sherwood. She had agreed with Jed that Sabrina needed to leave town, leave behind the ugly gossip and disturbing memories. "Do you really believe someone in town killed your parents?"

"Mother's last letter said Dad had given Chief Black Bear five steers to feed his tribe. Why would he kill the man who helped feed his tribe?"

She watched the mixture of pain and anger cross his face. "Do you have any other evidence?"

He shrugged his shoulders. "Enough to be suspicious."

Puzzled, Sabrina watched the countryside slowly roll by. Patrick had no one now. He was totally alone, and somehow the thought of being totally alone in the world sent a shiver of fear through her.

The Big C ranch house came into view, filling her with hope and expectation. Two years away from home and suddenly she could hardly contain herself. The last few steps of the horses seemed to take forever as Sabrina waited, impatient to be home.

Patrick halted the wagon in front of the weathered old house. Before he could help her out, Sabrina jumped down, anxious to see her family.

Roses climbed the porch railings, a living legacy from her mother. As she hurried up the steps, the blossoms swayed as she brushed them with her shoulder.

Sabrina threw open the front door just as her father came around the side of the house. "Sabrina? Is that you?"

At the sound of her father's voice, Sabrina turned. Releasing the front door, she hurried towards him. "Oh, Dad! What are you doing out of bed?"

Jed bounded up the porch steps and folded his arms around his daughter, engulfing her in his hug. "Damn, you're a welcome sight to these old eyes. But how did you know about my wound?"

Sabrina returned her father's welcoming hug. "I received your telegram. Now, answer my question."

"I'm fine. But I didn't send you no telegram." Jed released Sabrina and let his eyes wander over her. "Why didn't you let me know you were coming?"

"I wanted to surprise you, but I think you surprised me."

"That bullet grazed me, but didn't send me to my deathbed." Jed brushed a piece of hair off of her face.

Jed opened the door, and Sabrina reached out to stop him. "Dad, before we go in, could we talk for a few moments? Alone."

A puzzled expression crossed Jed's face. "Why, sure, hon. What's bother'n you?"

Sabrina glanced uneasily at her father, then at Patrick. She lowered her voice to a conspiratorial whisper. "Dad, if you didn't send me the telegram, who did? Could it have been Matt?"

Jed frowned at his daughter. "Matt didn't say anything about sending any telegram."

"Dad, the telegram also said—"

The door flew open and Sabrina watched the brother she loved stop in astonishment. Tall and blonde with sapphire eyes that matched her own, Matt had filled out and become a man. The memory of him standing in front of the judge made her shiver.

"Sabrina?"

He reached out and hugged his sister, spinning her around on the porch until she was dizzy.

"Matt! Put me down, you big lout"

Sabrina felt his body tense as he slowly released her. "Did *he* bring you home?"

She turned to Patrick, who was casually watching her. "Yes, Patrick brought me from town."

Her brother glared at Patrick, but said nothing more. Stepping back, he crossed his arms and leaned against the porch railing. God, would these two never get over that trial?

The memory of the last time they were all together was fresh in her mind. Reluctantly, she said, "Thanks for the ride."

Patrick nodded in brief acknowledgment. Feeling more tired than she'd felt the whole trip, she headed inside the house with Matt. Vaguely, she heard her father say, "Patrick, come on in."

"Thanks, Jed. I think I will."

Everyone followed Sabrina as she walked inside the house. A warm, safe feeling came over her as she stood looking around her home. Why had she waited so long to come back? Until this moment she hadn't realized how much she missed this place, but the telegram had warned her they were about to lose the ranch. Could it be true?

She moved toward the stairs, but stopped when her foot reached the first step. She had to know. She had waited almost three hundred miles and couldn't wait another second.